THE CUBICLE AT THE END

GUY M. ETCHELLS

To Suzanne

Thanks for your support.

Enjoy x

THE CUBICLE AT THE END

GUY M. ETCHELLS

Tower Hill Books

This is a work of fiction. Names, characters, places, and incidents either are the product of the author's imagination or are used fictitiously, and any resemblance to any persons, living or dead, business establishments, events, or locales is entirely coincidental.

First published in Great Britain by
Tower Hill Books
Copyright © 2024 Guy Etchells
All rights reserved

This paperback edition 2024
1

ISBN-13: 979-8874429577

The moral right of Guy Etchells to be identified as the author of this work has been asserted by him in accordance with the Copyright, Designs and Patents Act, 1988.

No part of this publication may be reproduced, stored in a retrieval system, or transmitted in any form or by any means, electronic, mechanical, photocopying, recording or otherwise without the prior written permission of the publishers.

This book may not be lent, hired out, resold or otherwise disposed of by any way of trade in any form of binding or cover other than that in which it is published, without the prior consent of the publishers.

For
Mom and Dad

A few days from now...

The woman's piercing scream echoed as she thrust her elbow into Scott's face, sending him stumbling backwards. A forceful sidekick struck his chest, leaving him sprawled on the floor, astonished by the fierce strength and agility of the young woman.

With a shriek, she targeted him again, launching herself into the air. Scott's instincts kicked in and he rolled to the right, narrowly avoiding her landing. She snarled and snapped at him like an animal, prompting him to rise and bolt for the safety of the open door.

The woman pursued him relentlessly, moving with an almost primal agility across the floor. With a burst of energy, she hurled herself through the air, wrapping her pale arms around his legs and bringing him down.

He fought back, kicking out as she clawed and thrashed, attempting to reach his vulnerable neck and face. He managed to seize her wrists and leveraging his strength, rolled her over, pinning her beneath him.

Despite her surprising strength, Scott, though a fit, young man recognised that her outward appearance of fragility could have easily misled him into underestimating her. As they locked eyes, he noticed a predatory glint, her lips curving into an anticipatory smile.

Expecting a bite or being spat at, he braced himself. Then, in a sudden shift, her muscles relaxed and she simply stared, her wide eyes exuding a menacing intensity. Scott's eyes blinked rapidly, unsettled by her unnaturally motionless state. A jolt ran through him. He sensed a presence, malevolent tendrils of her consciousness creeping in. She was there, probing and seizing control of his mind.

-1-

It was a busy Saturday night in the city.

Car horns, sirens, people laughing and screaming. Down a side street, litter blew around the entrance of the red-brick nightclub, Euphoria.

The neon yellow sign bathed the narrow street in an amber glow highlighting corrugated fast-food boxes and aluminium cans kicked about by the feet of burly doormen. Crowds lined up in a maze of ropes like a Skinner Maze waiting to gain entry to the building.

Inside, it resembled a 1980s brothel decorated with deep claret reds and shimmering golds. Dancers on podiums were lifted high above a dance floor teeming with moving bodies, swaying in a haze of dry ice and perspiration. The lower dance floor bar bustled with a crowd four or five bodies deep, while the music throbbed like the very pulse of the building.

From behind the bar, he spotted the girl immediately. She was with her friends again. This was getting too easy. He smiled, wiped his hands on some blue paper towel and manoeuvred past his work colleagues toward them.

'See you can't keep away?' he called over the music. 'What'll it be ladies?'

One of the three girls shouted over.

'A large white wine, double Bacardi and Coke and er... a double Vodka and Coke.'

'Can I guess which of you ladies is having which drink?'

'You're a bit cheeky, aren't you?'

'You're the Vodka and Coke, your blonde friend there is the Bacardi and you...' he stared at the girl with bronze, brown hair, 'are most definitely the white wine?'

The three girls screamed with laughter.

'I think we must be coming here a bit too often,' one of the girls cried.

He poured two drinks and then leaned over to the bronze-haired girl. 'You prefer a Sauvignon or a Pinot?'

He already knew the answer.'

'Sauvignon, please.'

'Okay, I just need to get some more out of the back.' He swiped a wine glass off the shelf and disappeared behind the bar.

He walked between boxes of stock. He used his keys to open the seal on a box containing six Sauvignon bottles. Carefully, he pulled out a tiny syringe from his pocket and injected its clear contents into the empty wine glass. He snapped the cap on a bottle and poured the wine out into the glass.

He listened.

He replaced the bottle in the box picked it up and placed it on his right arm balancing it against his chest. Retrieved the glass with his left hand and returned to the front bar.

It was busy. No one noticed he hadn't poured the wine there on the bar. He indicated with a nod and the box of bottles was taken away by a colleague.

With the box gone, he placed the large wine in front of the girl and smiled.

'Sorry to keep you waiting. Can I get you all free shots?'

***

An hour later, the three girls stood away from the dance floor in a corridor near the stairs to the upper floors.

'What the hell!' shouted, Jax, adjusting her ankle strap whilst holding onto the wall. 'Bloody hell, are you telling me, Josh has made a move at last?'

Tiff looked at the stunned expression on Amy and then back to Jax. 'Seriously,' Tiff squealed, 'I was there! I witnessed it. He asked her straight up.'

'Is change in life all it's cracked up to be? I guess we are about to find out,' Jax sang.

Amy spun around excitedly and flapped both hands like a baby bird.

Jax with her beautiful dark skin and huge deep rich eyes looked upon her two best buddies. Tiff, the dizzy curly blond whose idea of the real world was portrayed in reality shows that featured anyone from Essex, and Amy, a bronze-haired academic, a thoughtful play-it-safe girl, lacking confidence and hiding her beauty, unsure how to bring it out.

Jax saw it as her job to encourage Amy out of herself. They had enrolled at a new college where they had met and become friends. Tiff had joined the college in January for retakes and quickly they became the Billie Eilish Trio of the college common room.

Amy stopped flapping. 'You don't think it was a wind-up, do you?'

Tiff rolled her eyes. 'Anyway... so, what you need to do now is get yourself ready for a...' – she winked seductively – 'good night! Did you wax properly this time, the way I showed you?'

'Oh, sod off!' Amy threw her shoulders back as if preparing to deliver an Oscar award speech. 'I'll have you know, I'm fully functional and prepared in all those areas, my loyal bitches!'

They laughed.

'So, would you?' Tiff asked. 'I mean really. He is so into you. Did you see him bite his bottom lip when he asked you? I love it when a boy does that.'

Amy covered her face and moaned; her head had begun to spin.

'Don't worry chick, remember,' Tiff grinned, 'your mom thinks you're staying with me remember?'

Jax toppled forward pulling Amy's hands away from her face. 'You're going to get such a seeing to, young lady.' Jax sang, clicking her fingers around Amy's head diva style. 'More drinks, you bitches!'

'Whose round, is it?' Tiff asked confused.

'Yours!'

'Where are the others?'

'They're still dancing,' Jax said. She indicated down the red-carpeted corridor past groups of clubbers towards the dance area.

Amy raised a hand. 'Tiff you go, get drinks. Jax come with me, I need a wazz,' she laughed and attempted to walk away without swaying.

Jax grinned. 'Don't think I've ever heard Amy say the word *wazz*. Check her out, she's only had a couple of wines and a shot. Now, Tiff, I want you to listen to me.'

'What?'

'Go to the right-hand side of the bottom bar. The cute security guy stands there. He'll make sure you're served.'

'Oh, you mean Mr Chunky Monkey?'

'Yes, Mr Chunky Monkey.'

'Oh, the things he could do to me.' Tiff giggled opening her handbag. 'Oh, yeah I need money, don't I?'

Jax pouted. 'Go, go, go. Meet you back here.'

***

In the sumptuous second-floor restroom, Amy held her phone as steady as she could. She pressed the camera button. There was a click, a pause and she half laughed/half groaned. 'Oh, my vision is everywhere. Hell! I've never felt this pissed before. Feels weird.'

Jax held her by the shoulders and guided her through a sea of women, perfume and potential tantrums.

'God, I'm twatted!' Jax shouted.

'Not far behind you, mate. Oh hell! The cubicles are all engaged.'

'Over here. The last one isn't,' called Jax.

Amy stumbled to the last cubicle throwing her phone into her handbag. She stared at a battered old door. 'I ain't going in there!' She eyed the other occupied cubicles with their arctic white panels. 'Oooooh, but I can't hold on much longer.'

Jax opened the door and pushed her in. 'In, in, piss, girl, piss.' Jax turned to the nearest mirror, 'I wish Tiff weren't so bloody timid, she'll take ages getting served, bless her.

At a sink, warm water cascaded over Jax's hands. As she moved to the hand dryer it unleashed a blast of hot air down her arms and wisped at her hair. The noise faltered when she took a step back, leaving behind a momentary hush.

'God, this mirror makes me look like shit.' She fumbled for her makeup listening to Amy giggling behind the cubicle door, 'What's so funny?'

'You, Jax! You have the look and body of a movie star. You never look like shit. I, however, look trashed,' she paused. 'What you gonna do if I go back with Josh?'

Jax drew her lipstick over her top lip 'What? Little old me, I think I'm going after Squid.'

'Squid, again?'

'Again, I'm going to ride him till his eyes roll back and his knees buckle. He'll think his birthday's come early.'

'But you said he couldn't get hard last time and you'd never go there again!' shrieked Amy.

'Girl, I'll bloody... think of something. Never underestimate the powers of Madam Jacqueline. I'll get that thing up if I have to make a splint.'

'You're a dangerous girl, Jax!'

'Says the girl who's going to get action all night with a guy the size of a brick shithouse.'

'Have you seen the size of his legs?' Amy asked.

No one noticed the incessant hum of the extraction fans discreetly nestled within the walls go silent, or the subtle tremor course through the air, causing an imperceptible flicker to dance across the surface of every phone screen.

Jax laughed as she adjusted her hair and performed the practised pout at her reflection. She scanned the room at all the girls filling the already cramped area. Jax gathered herself and stepped over to Amy's cubicle door. 'Oh shit, Amy, Tanya tiny-tits just walked in.'

Jax could hear Amy giggle once more.

'Just think nice thoughts, Jax.' Amy whispered. 'And why is it so bloody cold in here? I feel really...'

Jax folded her arms. 'I can't see why anyone would want to even look at Tanya Benson. You should wait till you see what she's wearing. Holy crap! She's got her chav mates with her. You know, the ones whose sister went missing at Christmas. The Police still haven't got a clue.' Jax stretched both arms out and yawned. 'Her family probably ate her.'

A faint blue light began to emanate from beneath Amy's cubicle door, reminiscent of the ambient light emitted from a tanning bed.

Jax started picking at her nails, head down looking through her eyelashes at the other girls.

'On Facebook, right, she claims to be seeing that fit guy off the market store. You know the one I mean?' She said grinning, 'The one I like. He's so cute in a rugged way with hands the size of dinner plates,' Jax shuddered. Standing upright, she quickly looked around nervously, 'Flippineck! It's getting bloody cold in here. Amy hurry up will ya! Have they got air-con in here now or what?'

Jax scanned the ceiling looking for a device that would explain the sudden chill. She noticed other women reacting in the same way. 'Is it me or is life just getting weirder the older we get?'

The cold disappeared, replaced with a surge of warmth that returned like air from a vent. The atmosphere grew heavy again with the scent of perfumes, deodorants, and the subtle tang of sweat

The dormant extraction fans whispered back to life.

Jax leaned back, throwing a menacing scowl at Tanya, who was now surrounded by an entourage of new gaggling women. 'Market-man can't fancy her... bitch! My cat's got bigger tits than her.'

A loud beep made her jump. She reached for her phone and tapped on the screen loving the click her nails made on the surface. 'The others are asking where we are, wait...

Lola's here and she's been... OMG! She's been sick, lightweight, we gotta see this. Come on Amy... Amy?'

Jax knocked on the cubicle door. 'You okay babe? Come on, Josh's gonna lose interest... Amy?' Jax knocked on the door harder this time, not caring if the other women could hear. 'Amy, what's wrong? Answer me or I'll kick the soddin' door in, I'm serious. Shit!'

Frantically she looked at the crowd of women. Gone was the tough exterior and confident Jax. In its place, a frightened girl unsure, her brain scrambled.

'Can somebody go and get help – get security!' She shouted at them frantically. 'I think my friend passed out or something... please!'

Jax spun round to the door her fist hammering on the battered crumbling surface. She tried the latch but withdrew her hand nurturing it confused.

'It's freezing!'

Panicked, some of the women fled the room. Some muttering about drugs. Others clung together and continued to stare.

'Amy, open the door for Christ's sake! You're scaring me, babe.'

'Click!'

The sound came from the latch on the cubicle door. Jax looked down to see the dial now reading vacant.

She took one step back. Her left arm tentatively stretched out not wanting to open the door for fear of finding the worst. Before she could touch it, the door swung inward to reveal an empty cubicle.

Jax stepped forward.

Pieces of toilet paper stuck to a damp floor.

Cigarette ash lay on top of the cistern and a couple of dried leaves had collected around a stained white sanitary bin.

Amy was gone.

-2-

For pensioner, Rosemary Moon with her short winter white hair, twinkling eyes and cotton handkerchief, it had been a busy day. But nothing worked better for solving problems than keeping busy.

She placed the damp tea towel on the kitchen radiator and sighed deeply. Something bothered her.

At sixty-eight, she thought she would care a lot less about things and at least begin to take life easier.

Her daily routine would have put anyone to shame, and it certainly intimidated her daughter, Carol.

Up at first light, she would fill every waking moment with a rich mix of meeting friends, reading and coffee mornings. Additionally, she had her social club, a part-time cleaning job and above all else, she had paranormal investigating.

The last one was a big secret. Her daughter, Carol, had no clue what her mother and father had gotten up to throughout the years. If Carol did suspect, then she had kept quiet, which for Carol would have been quite an accomplishment.

Hearing footsteps upstairs, Rosemary moved into the cluttered lounge. She sat on her preferred chair and began directing the remote control at the television.

Carol walked in and put a mug of tea in front of her mother with a grunt.

'You left that upstairs, it's almost cold.' She jangled a set of keys and headed to the dining table.

Rosemary gave up stabbing at the remote and looked at her mug with a Christmas robin design on it. She remembered how her grandson, George, had presented her with the mug wrapped in Star Wars paper two years previous. It was not Christmas now, but Rosemary was convinced in her mind that this mug made her tea taste better.

'Ooh, thanks luv. I don't mind if it's cold as long as it's wet. What are you looking for?'

'My mobile, I keep losing the bloody thing,' Carol huffed.

'Mind your language, young lady! It is late. What do you need it for now anyway?'

Carol placed both hands on her hips. She scanned the room for the third time, '...picking George, up, aren't I? It's almost ten-thirty.'

'Oh yes luv, I remember now. Can't one of the other mothers at the school pick him up?' Rosemary asked. She tried to twist around to look at her daughter. She knew Carol's irate voice. 'What about little Omar's parents, with the nice car?'

'No Mom! I'm supposed to be the one picking Omar up too. Didn't you hear me tell you all this earlier? You never listen to me.'

Rosemary turned back to the television. 'On my own again then.'

'Don't start Mom! I'll just be over an hour... Do you think I want to drive out at this time of the night? And in this rain? You'll be in bed with PD James anyway.'

Carol continued the search. She moved to the bookshelf covered with dog ornaments and framed pictures of the family.

'Oh, I remember school trips as a girl,' Rosemary chuckled ignoring her daughter, 'They were the highlight of the year in my day. But isn't it a bit late to be dropping off students?' Without moving her gaze off the remote, Rosemary stretched over with her right hand. She lifted a corduroy brown cushion that had seen better days. Under it lay a mobile phone.

'The school coach has been stuck in traffic on the soddin motorway for nearly two hours!' Carol replied leaning over the back of the settee and snatching the mobile without so much as a thank you. 'Bet he ain't had anything to eat.' She grabbed her coat off a dining room chair.'

Rosemary glanced at her. 'You should learn to hang that up.'

'Mother! How old am I?'

'Thirty-five, dear.'

Carol frantically buttoned up her coat. 'Oh, I nearly forgot, the nightclub rang, they want you to work over tomorrow. Something to do with one of the other cleaners having a hospital appointment. I told them you'd ring them back before bed.'

Rosemary pulled off her glasses. 'Do you know who it was that rang? Did you get a name? Have you written it down?'

'No, Mom! I had the phone in one hand, and thanks to my comical son I managed to pour Ozma's cat litter into the cereal bowl, which he'll find hilarious... and then, that same button decided to pop off my blouse! You know my favourite Marks & Spencer's animal print blouse with the bishop sleeves?'

'I never did like that blouse, makes you look like a Jezebel.'

Carol ignored her mother and breathed out slowly, 'I'll see you when I get back if you're still up.'

She stood unmoving for a few moments lost in thought, then threw herself out into the hall and out the front door.

Rosemary sighed and without replacing her glasses, she looked at the remote, pointed and pressed. She smiled as the title theme for *Murder, She Wrote* swamped the room.

She got up, walked to the window and pulled the net curtain slightly. She watched Carol's car drive away down the street.

Now she could get to work. She went to the side cupboard, retrieved her knitting bag and returned to the sofa. She emptied its contents. At the bottom of the bag, she pulled out an unusual gadget. It looked like an old radio with extra bits of metal and switches.

'Even something old can be made good again. The old rejuvenated in remarkable ways,' she whispered. 'All you have to do is to want it.'

With a twinkle in her eye, she carefully took a screwdriver hidden amongst her knitting needles and started to tinker.

-3-

Scott Finn woke to the sound of screaming. His vision struggling, he caught movement in the corner of the room. He blinked rapidly and waited for his eyes to adjust. It was a nurse. He was in a hospital and his head hurt.

Sounds were whispering around in his mind. A mass of voices, like being at a party or a train station. Voices that made no sense because there were too many of them, all forced together and pushed inside his skull. Four weeks now, he thought. Four weeks of waking like this. Feeling disorientated for minutes every morning, and the pain and whispering hadn't stopped.

He concentrated and breathed slowly as he'd been taught to do.

The sounds faded like breath on a winter morning. He moved slightly attracting the attention of the nurse who came to his side.

'Oh, good morning. Did that scream wake you up? Not to worry, someone's just been brought in and not too happy by the sound of it,' she whispered with a smile.

'What hospital am I in?' Scott pushed back his dark chin-length hair off his face and rubbed his stubble. He scanned the room and coughed. His throat felt dry and scratchy like a fibre breakfast.

'You said the same thing yesterday and the day before that,' answered the nurse.

Scott's gaze met hers, finding a woman with dark-cropped hair. She appeared to be middle-aged, possessing a gentle countenance and a slight plumpness. She wore a conspicuous yellow badge bearing the inscription: Evelyn Middleton.

'How are you feeling?' Her voice was soft. 'Feel any change from yesterday?'

She took the water jug off the side cabinet and walked to the bathroom. 'The nightshift staff said you haven't been sleeping... not surprising really. Have you regained any memories about the accident yet?'

'Accident? No... I... I don't...' Scott trailed off. He felt stupid.

She returned with fresh water.

'Well, I'll let the doctor know you're awake.' She looked at her fob watch attached to her uniform. 'It's Doctor Phaedrus this morning. She's lovely. She'll be on her rounds now, so shouldn't be too long and the catering assistant will be in with breakfast in a second.'

Nurse Middleton was becoming familiar as Scott caught a scent that drifted down from a memory. Estee Lauder talc. He knew the name and the smell. It was comforting.

The nurse adjusted the blinds. The water jug on the cabinet caught the sun, casting shards of light across the walls.

'So, nothing floating up in the memory of yours yet?' Anything about leaky pipes, blocked restrooms or heating ducts? You are a plumber, aren't you,' she jabbed a finger toward him, 'Can you tell me who the Prime Minister is?'

Scott fidgeted awkwardly. 'Erm, no I can't right now, I really can't. Have I lost my memory? Is that why I'm here?'

'No, no... you've just lost some memories, that's all, but they'll come back in time. They always do, so don't you worry.'

'I see faces flashing up in my head,' Scott said. He was beginning to feel anxious, a tightening in the chest crushing him. His breathing got quicker as images of places and events swept through his mind.

Nurse Middleton was there at his side. She placed her hand on his. It felt warm and soft. 'These things take time. Don't worry too much.'

'I can't give it time! This feels all messed up. It feels wrong. Where exactly am I?'

'Don't worry about that now. Can you tell me what your name is?' She asked.

Scott looked away from her and pondered for a moment.

'Why do I not know who I am?' Scott felt flustered, tears stinging his eyes. 'I can't be like this. Why is this happening? I just want to get out of here.' He concentrated and breathed slowly. 'I just want to go and eat chips, get drunk, go to work. Why can I remember chips but not my name? What happened to me?'

Nurse Middleton's face changed from kindness to concern. She quickly turned her head scanning the room in twitchy movements that reminded Scott of a garden sparrow.

Her gaze fell on the door where it stayed fixed. 'I must go... he's coming,' she said, darkly.

'Who?' Scott unconsciously grasped the crisp white sheet that lay across his body. 'The doctor? You mean the doctor's coming? I thought you said the doctor was a woman. Will she know what's wrong with me?'

Nurse Middleton spun round to face him her palms up. 'Just accept who you are, luv. Stop fighting. It's the only way.' The nurse hesitated. Then after checking her appearance, she hurried out of the room, leaving behind Estee Lauder and dancing light on walls.

Confused, Scott glanced around the room before he swung his warm legs out from under the sheet. The bed creaked, fracturing the eerie silence. He sat up and stretched.

He noticed a large brown cardboard box lying on the floor. It looked so out of place. The open flaps of the box spread out like a starfish.

A memory floated through his mind. When he was a boy, he had asked his parents to bring back empty boxes from the local supermarket. With them, he could create space stations for his action figures. Boxes and cardboard tubes, cotton reels and the smell of grease... a garage with a workbench.

He smiled and lowered himself to the cold floor. Hesitantly, he approached the box unsure why it was there. He held his breath and kicked one side of the box.

It sounded hollow.

He relaxed understanding how stupid he was being. It was just a box. He felt clumsy and weak. He turned, stepping back to the bed rubbing both hands over his face feeling stubble and a scar on his cheek. He drove his fingers through his long hair and sighed. He tapped his fingers on the bed's metal headrest just to make some noise. He paused, feeling the urge to look back at the box. No, not an urge, more an instinct.

Scott glanced over his shoulder.

The box had vanished.

Delicate snowflakes drifted down through the room. He stepped back blinking and began to shiver.

A presence seeped into the room.

It lurked in the corner. A towering figure stretching seven feet tall, dark, chitinous, sleek, limbs extending into long appendages tipped with spike-like digits. At its head rested the cardboard box concealing its features. The flaps of the box lay across its shoulders and chest. With a deliberate, scraping motion against the wall, it began to pivot, its perception acutely attuned to his presence.

Every nerve in Scott's body was on edge.

A parched, raspy sound emanated from beneath the box.

Scott screamed.

***

He opened his eyes feeling woozy and uncertain, breathing fast. He was in his bedroom apartment. The curtains were drawn but the morning light streamed in through a crack. He threw the covers off and swung his legs out.

Two delicate arms wrapped around him from behind and squeezed. He turned around to face a young woman with dark hair.

'Hey, another dream?' Annie's eyes narrowed.

Scott wriggled free and stood.

'Er yeah... it's nothing. You know what the doctor said, bad dreams and all that. It's to be expected.'

Annie smiled softly. 'Still battling who you are, eh? You know that's the reason why you're having these nightmares.'

Scott glanced down at her Marvel comics t-shirt. How she loved that shirt. This was Annie. He knew her somehow. He felt safe with her.

'You understand that you can't go back to the way you were. That old life is not the direction you need to head. It's not your path. You do know that, don't you?'

Scott focused on Annie's chestnut eyes and shrugged. 'What are you on about, Annie? What do you mean? Who cares? It's morning and I need a glass of water.'

Annie sighed and flopped onto the bed smiling. 'You do realise that waking up in a hospital with no memory is very cliché these days? Anyway, I'll say it again. I think you're going to be something special, Scotty Finn.'

He shook his head and indicated to the clock on the side. 'I won't be special if I don't get to price this job. I'm supposed to give a quote in the next two hours.'

Scott stretched. He enjoyed the feel of his muscles finding flexibility again. 'Waking up in the hospital with no memory? That's only in my nightmares. I woke up on some grass bank and then found my way to a hospital.'

Annie leaned forward. 'The doctor said it was a type of memory loss.'

Scott laughed dryly. 'Yes, I know. I can still drive my van, thankfully. They didn't take my license away. I can still play footie, order a burger and stuff. It's just... well, it's just certain people that I've forgotten and little bits of world history.'

'Oh, come on... a little bit of world history. Thank heavens there aren't two of you to cope with. Oh, and that reminds me, last night your room was lit up like a beacon again. Do you have some ultraviolet lighting somewhere? Annie asked with a smile. 'The whole wall was literally all white this time.'

Scott turned away snatching his dressing gown off the floor and headed for the bedroom door. 'Once again, I don't know what you're talking about, I didn't get woken up. It's probably someone in the opposite building. You know with one of those light sources for recording YouTube or something. Forget the glass of water, I'll go put the kettle on. I suppose you want a quick cuppa before I go?'

There was no reply.

He leaned against the frame his head down. 'You've gone again, haven't you?'

No reply.

The room was empty.

He was alone.

-4-

Rosemary walked into the manager's office of Euphoria; it was early morning.

As a cleaner at the nightclub, she had often wished for the opportunity to clean the claustrophobic office, with its dusty 1970s Venetian-style blinds and worn swirly patterned ochre carpet. The walls were lined with boxes which made it even smaller.

Amongst the litter of papers, used coffee mugs and beer glasses sat Maria Gilbert otherwise known to the staff as Guillotine-Gil. It was easy to see why. Short sharp black hair, face thin pale and stressed beyond her years.

'Damn it!' she muttered with an exasperated sigh. Maria tried again to get her second earring in.

Rosemary watched Maria push too hard; the resulting pain in Maria's face made Rosemary wince.

Maria slammed down the earring.

'What?' Maria spat out without looking up.

Rosemary smiled to herself and tucked her hands into her checked tabard.

Maria sighed heavily and looked up.

'Rosemary, good morning or rather just morning. I've asked each member of staff to pop into the office before their shift starts. I want you to get the story direct from me. No point calling a meeting as you're all in at different bloody times thanks to Dan's rota. You know what they're like here for gossip. So yes, before you ask... another girl went missing. Police have been here all night as you've probably heard. So, I need you to start cleaning all floors as normal. The police say it's okay now they've finished with their initial investigation.' She stood, pushing back the chair with the backs of her knees. She walked over to the filing cabinet. 'You're the only cleaner in today with Frank off.'

'Only me!' Rosemary exclaimed.

'Is that okay?' Maria asked without hesitating, 'and we weren't able to clear up the meeting rooms in time either.

So can you strip the tablecloths off and take them to the laundry room.'

'But they're heavy!'

'Just get one of the lads off the bar to help you with them.'

Rosemary pulled out a handkerchief and wiped her left eye. 'Oh well, yes. I guess I'll be alright. Who's off with a hospital appointment then?'

'Natalie. She had authorised it with Dan, but he forgot to cover the shift. None of the others could cover at such short notice. We may need to get casual cover staff at this rate.'

Rosemary adjusted her tabard. 'Well, yes, I'll be okay doing a few more hours. I told Carol I'd get the bus back as I didn't know what time I'd–'

'Carol?' Maria asked slamming the cabinet shut.

Rosemary rolled her eyes. 'My daughter!'

'Oh yes. The place is a bombsite, Rosemary, so I want you to begin sorting out as much as you can. The bar staff... I think Shaun and Neil are on the top floor. They have already cleaned that level. But may need you to throw the vacuum around.'

She jabbed a finger at Rosemary. 'Contractors and plumbers are coming in throughout the morning. They're here to give us quotes on structural stuff, you know for the lighting rigs and that ongoing problem with the restrooms. So don't panic if you see strange people walking around, I know what you're like for questioning new people.'

Rosemary stepped to one side as Maria took a file and moved around the desk.

'It'll be nice to see some lovely young men around. Rosemary chuckled attempting to lighten the mood in the tiny office. 'I don't get to see many at my age.'

Maria ignored her.

Rosemary turned to leave.

'Bring us a coffee, will you, Rosemary? Before you start.'

***

A white 2018 transit van reversed between a 2002 blue Fiat Punto and an overflowing yellow skip near Euphoria. The side of the van read Finn's Eco-plumbing.

Inside, Scott sat in the drivers seat staring at the dashboard, deep in thought. The windows had already steamed up and it was getting cold. His mobile rang breaking the silence.

'Finn's? Oh hi... Dad. No, no. I'm about to go in, I'm a bit early luckily traffic was good.' He leaned over releasing his seatbelt, 'Dad, no, I've got to price another job tomorrow. Yeah, a good one if I get it. At least two months' work. Probably, yeah. Most of the morning down in Colesworth so no, I doubt I'll be around Monday daytime so tell... er... Mom okay?. Yes, I know how to get to Colesworth... stop worrying, the consultant said it's my personal identity that's gone, not my sense of direction. Are we still on for getting chips tonight? Alright, Dad... I'll see you later. Okay... bye.'

Scott paused and closed his eyes listening to his breathing. He tossed his mobile into the glove compartment and slammed it shut, took the keys out of the ignition, locked his steering wheel and got out.

***

An hour and a half later, Rosemary wearily entered the ladies' restroom on the first floor, pushing her cleaning trolley. She leaned back out the door and glanced up and down the corridor.

All clear.

Rosemary furrowed her brow and straightened.

'What have you got for me today?'

She rubbed her hands. She reached to a shelf on her trolley and uncovered the radio-like gadget she had been working on. She activated it as she passed the rows of cubicles.

It hissed and hummed.

She glanced from the radio to each cubicle as she passed. At the cubicle at the end, the radio erupted, screeching and bleeping. She paused, then pushed open the battered door.

'Definitely, this cubicle every single time.' Rosemary looked around the small space, still managing to tap away on the device. She began to turn in a complete circle. Everything was familiar. Nothing unusual after a busy Saturday night.

But her eyes widened at the dried leaves collected around the sanitary bin.

She completed her turn and noticed more dried leaves lying at the side of the restroom. They had not been there a moment ago. She took a deep breath.

She stepped away.

It was not the first time she had seen these types of leaves here.

'Rosemary to reception please, Rosemary to reception!' Maria's voice boomed over the club tannoy system.

'Bloody woman! If women are going missing, I wish someone would take her. Can't she leave me alone for five minutes?' Rosemary muttered. She hid her device back in the cleaning trolley before she walked out of the restroom.

***

In her flight from the room, Rosemary did not see the blue glow of light begin to emanate at the bottom of the door of the last cubicle. Her radio device, hidden beneath the trolley, crackled into life and began a mournful wail. The faint glow flared up briefly. It then died back leaving only darkness below the door.

-5-

There was something about the dark-haired visitor in reception that caught Rosemary's attention. It was not the stubbled face or the long hair tied back in a half man-bun. It wasn't even the military green jacket he removed to reveal a black polo t-shirt. It was something discordant, something that made her think that he did not belong here. She made a mental note of the company logo, *Finn's Eco-Plumbing*, embroidered on his t-shirt and the large tool bag he carried.

Maria smiled, which unnerved Rosemary.

'Rosemary, this is Scott, he's come to give us a quote on a few plumbing matters I've outlined for him. Could you please show him where the restrooms are on all levels and the kitchen? I've explained the problems we've been having. I've opened the emergency escape doors to the yard so he and any other contractors can get to their vans. Is that okay?'

'Why me? I've still got two restrooms and a dance floor to do?'

'Rosemary, I'm doing the wages, so if you want to get paid on time, you'll do it!' She gave a half-smile.

Noting the edge in Maria's voice, the plumber stepped forward and extended his hand to Rosemary.

'Ello, Rosemary. It shouldn't take long.'

The moment she took his hand, she knew. It was like she had drunk a whole jug of lemonade too fast. She could feel the bubbles in her chest and down to her stomach. She found it difficult to hold back the smile.

'Yes, yes indeed, this is good, well, if you'd like to come this way, Scott, is it? I'm not very good with names.'

***

In the ladies' restroom door on the first floor, the strange old lady pulled Scott through. She checked behind her in the hallway before closing the door. She pulled the cleaning trolley across to prevent exit.

'An early warning system,' she whispered.

Scott watched as the woman's demeanour changed. The slow walk and slight waddle were gone. Her bent-over posture was replaced with a straight back and a chin held high. He dropped his tool bag and watched as she confidently strode down the rows of cubicle doors. He wondered if it was just him.

'...and this is the ladies' restroom, level one.'

Scott looked from the cleaner back to the door. 'Er... yeah, I worked that one out.'

The woman rubbed her hands together, the hiss of palm against palm the loudest noise in the room.

'Let's begin by getting a few ground rules straight just so we get things running smoothly. An operant outranks a specialist. This is my investigation, so you'll follow my lead and not place yourself in danger.'

Scott stared at the cleaner.

'The phenomenon is located here at this end cubicle,' she continued. 'No surprise, I mean just look at the state of it! It screams creepy. May as well place a huge neon sign above it that says, 'supernatural lives here'.'

'When you say phenomenon, you mean the worst of the leaks you've been having?' Scott asked raising an eyebrow.

The woman ignored him.

'Now, I've analysed the door on this particular cubicle at regular intervals.' She swept her palms over the door. 'It's made of actual wood and only coated in a cheap plastic, unlike the others in here which are comprised of a modern composite – you know the traditional high-pressure laminate with a chipboard core!'

'I know what high-pressure laminate is, luv,' Scott replied.

The woman simply waved her hands. 'There's a temperature drop here as well that seems to be increasing in size of late, which is a bit worrying. It's the reason I felt the need to contact you.'

'Are you having a laugh, luv?'

'I'm sorry?' the woman said, turning her head to the side. 'Oh, very funny, but you can drop the act, we're the only ones on this floor.' Smiling she walked up to, Scott. 'I hid a doorway charm at the top of the stairs. It'll last about another hour. Now, hold out your hand and tell me about this.'

The cleaner removed a single dried red leaf from the pocket of her tabard. 'It's not an afterimage or a projection, it's real. It exists in the here and now. However, it took me a while to pluck up the courage to touch it.'

'It's a leaf.' Scott cocked an eyebrow.

'This isn't the only one, sunshine,' she indicated to the floor spreading her palms outward. 'They appear at random. I can't think for the life of me where they are all coming from. I clean in here. I check the vents, every outlet. There is no natural way they could have gotten in. They simply keep coming back. There's sometimes, two or three, sometimes more.' She nodded quickly. 'Go on then, what are you waiting for!' She held out the leaf. 'Take it, *psychometry* was never my strong point.'

'Look, love, I'm all for equal opportunity and helping those with... well, those who need help, but I need to get on.'

Scott collected his tool bag and brushed past the old woman. He placed his bag on the sink area and started to remove panels from beneath to gain access. He saw the cleaner steeple her hands together from the corner of his eye.

'I know what you're doing... silly me, silly old, Rosemary. Even so, I did think that after all the years I'd given to the department, all the work I'd put in and despite our differences, they'd skip protocol. But I guess the Ministry of Defence still thinks very highly of me because, well... here you are!'

Scott ignored her hoping desperately that she would leave.

'Why are you examining the pipes?'

He heard her wrap her knuckles on the cubicle's discoloured, cracked surface.

'The energy is localised here in this cubicle. Are you listening to me? I've been keeping the department updated with regular emails on all my findings from the investigation. Were you not briefed? This is serious. Four girls are missing! One only last night.'

'That's it!' Scott swiped his hand at the cleaner trying to whisper. 'Can you just shut the hell up! I ain't got time to talk to some batty old women about shit. I need this job, okay? If your boss lady downstairs wants to know where I am, tell her I'm starting in the men's restroom on the top floor. I'll find my way!'

Scott snatched his tool bag and leaving the open panels on the floor he stood, pushed the trolley to the wall with a bang and walked out.

***

Scott had started work in the men's restroom. It was painted an off-white; the floor was tiled grey and the smell of urine hung in the air, it reminded him of something, but it was like grabbing at fog. Then the memory of the nightmares and the figure with the box covering its head crept back into his thoughts but he didn't know why.

He shook his head. He had seen some horrendous bathrooms in his time, he seemed to remember that. He could recall some of them, but not all and this was what frustrated him the most.

Why would he remember specific things and have no memory of others? He caught his reflection in the mirror and cringed. This was still so strange to him, seeing the face looking back at him. It must be what it is like to wake up after facial reconstruction.

He got down and removed another panel from beneath the nearest sink. He crawled underneath and began tracing the pipes through the system. He would need to see what set-up they had here, then remove some ceiling tiles and get up above the bathrooms to discover the leaks. He'd have to get the step ladders at some point from his van, but the thought of colliding with the crazy cleaner put him off.

A female voice came from above him.

'The Ministry of Defence, didn't send you, did they?'

Scott sighed. He pulled himself from beneath the sink and raised his hand. 'Look, luv, I don't know what the hell you're on about. I'm a plumber. This is my job, I help myself, I look after myself, and I mind my own business.'

He disappeared back beneath the sink.

'But you're not only a plumber, are you?' Rosemary insisted, edging nearer.

'No, I'm supposed to be a son. I'm someone who likes fish and chips, who watches Sky News. Apparently, I have an X-BOX, drink pints of bitter and I grew my hair after watching *Lord of the Rings*. Now, how about you let me get on before I have a word with your boss?'

The cleaner narrowed her eyes. 'But I shook your hand downstairs.'

'Well, thank you very much for that,' replied Scott. 'Don't mean we're married. What mental home did they get you from?'

'No, no, shaking your hand, it told me about you. You're like me.'

Scott drew back slightly as the woman turned round in a full circle holding her hands over her mouth. 'Oh, bless you. You don't know, do you? Or perhaps you just don't want to know.'

Scott had had enough. He stood up and folded his arms. 'Okay, I don't mean to be rude lady but I'm going to have a word with your boss!'

'You're psychic, a paranormal.'

He heard her say the words quietly.

'You're like me... I mean, so am I, although... I'm not a particularly strong one. But you... you, on the other hand.'

He watched the cleaner push her hands deep into her tabard pockets. 'How could I have got this so wrong? I just thought that some friends of mine had sent you, to help. I guess... I guess they're still not getting my messages or they just don't want to talk to me.'

Scott acknowledged the woman as she gave him a half-hearted smile.

'I'm sorry to have troubled you, son. I won't be bothering you again.'

Scott remained watching the cleaner slowly turn and walk out. Not the upright, confident woman he had witnessed before, but a weary woman, deflated and sad.

-6-

That evening Rosemary's mood was solemn as she sat on the edge of her bed. She liked how the streetlamp illuminated her dark, warm bedroom with a comforting amber glow and the muffled sounds that came from downstairs. The television was on and she could hear the clatter of dishes in the kitchen.

On the dresser, Rosemary pushed aside her makeup bag and a strange iridescent blue bottle, revealing a silver-framed picture. It showed a white-haired, handsome man in brown trousers and a white shirt. He held a pot of scarlet tulips and yellow narcissus. He stood in a garden surrounded by bluebells and snowdrops. Above him, a blue sky peppered with fluffy white clouds. That day he had given her the old iridescent bottle, the memory remained etched in mind, a relic that stood sentinel-like on her dresser ever since. Not every man expressed love by gifting their wife a witch bottle.

She had lost count of the number of times she had spoken to his picture sitting there on the same corner of the bed. So many conversations with Henry James Moon and for the first time in memory she did not know what to say. That is what she was attempting now, asking Henry what she should do. She would hear his voice advising her. She knew what he would tell her as clearly as if he were sitting right next to her.

'Rosemary, you're getting too old for all this... let it go, luv, you've done your bit, you've done enough.'

There was a light knock at her door.

Carol walked in carrying a pile of folded clothes. She placed them on the bed after clicking the light switch on with her elbow.

'What are you doing sitting in the dark? Didn't you hear me shouting? Casualty's about to start.'

Rosemary breathed out quickly. 'Okay luv, can you help me up, I've seized up a bit.'

Carol gently took her mum by the arm and helped her off the bed.

'Don't forget, you've got four episodes of *NCSI* recorded as well. Why you watch them, I've no idea. You don't strike me as a Sherlock Holmes type. I hope you're not getting ideas again about tackling crime and wrestling jewellery thieves like Dad used to. He was a bit too obsessed with crime shows for my liking.'

Carol crossed the room and closed the curtains. 'There you go. Now you find your slippers and I'll run down and put the kettle on. We'll only miss the first bit.'

Rosemary retrieved her warmed slippers off the radiator next to her dresser. She glanced at Henry's picture.

'Maybe you're right, luv,' she whispered. 'After this mystery, I believe it's time to bow out, leave it to the young ones, eh?' She paused and touched the picture before switching off the bedroom light and making her way downstairs.

***

Scott opened the car door and eased himself into the plush BMW, glad to be out of the chilly, damp night. He looked across at his dad, Graham Finn, with his grey hair, receding hair line and glasses.

Graham smiled back and lowered the volume on the opera playing through the high-end sound system. As Scott gently placed his phone on the luxurious dashboard, his fingers instinctively caressed the supple leather seats.

With a purr, the BMW's engine roared to life and Graham pulled away. It was not difficult to see the similarities between the two men. The strong nose, deep brown eyes, thick dark eyebrows and square jawline.

'Thanks for picking me up. Bit posh this, ain't it! How long have you had this then?' Scott asked checking out the back seat.

'Two years now.' Graham replied after a short pause.

'It's nice, a bit of a change from my van,' Scott said.

'Your mother doesn't like it much.'

'Really, why?'

'She struggles to get in and out of it,' Graham raised an eyebrow, 'complains it's too low.'

'Oh, I see,' Scott said.

'Good news about your driver's licence, son. I thought you'd get at least a temporary suspension.'

'Yeah, it is good news. They said I still met the requirements for safe driving and as I've never had an episode before they wouldn't revoke my licence this time.'

'Your mom was worried about how you were going to get to work without the van.'

'Oh! I might have a job over in Colesworth!'

'That's great, well done,' Graham chuckled. 'What is it? apartments, house, a brothel?'

'Nightclub, so same thing I guess,' Scott smiled, 'Starting it tomorrow morning. It seems a really old place, I guess it must have been something in its day. A lot of stuff going wrong, an old water system and a lot of water damage.'

'Oh, well, it'll keep you busy.'

'They just want a patch-up job, but it's steady work for a week or two.'

'And you're feeling alright about being back at work?' Graham asked.

'I get some looks when people ask me stuff. They think I'm a bit thick.'

'Surely not. Anyway, there's a lot of old buildings over in Colesworth, you know? It managed to avoid a lot of bombing back in the war, so a lot is still standing.'

Scott turned. 'War?'

'Oh, ahh, sorry yes, well, we've had a couple. Second World War, I think. Your grandfather, on your mum's side, worked in Colesworth in the library there for most of his life I believe. You'll have to ask her.'

'Wars?' Scott shook his head and looked out the window.

'How are you sleeping? Your mother wanted me to ask.'

'Not good but tell her I'm not ready for chamomile tea just yet.'

'I don't think either of us will be ready for chamomile tea, but you know what she's like.'

'No, not really, but tell her, I'm doing better. I don't want her to worry.'

'That's like telling a duck not to quack.' Graham signalled and took the first exit off the ring road. They drove in silence for a while, then stopped off at a local fish and chip shop.

On the way back, Scott began tapping on the dashboard.

'Dad?'

'Son?'

'Am I different now? I mean – am I changed – more unusual than I was before the incident?'

Graham remained expressionless considering the question as he pulled away at the traffic lights.

'I won't lie to you, son. Yes, you are.'

Scott looked away again and watched the lights in people's houses. He wondered what stories each house held and whether they were as strange as his.

'Have you thought any more about moving back with me and your mother for a bit? Just to be on the safe side?'

'Nah! Not just yet, eh? I'll see how it goes, now I'm back at work. Thanks anyway.'

'Okay, son. Well, here we are,' Graham said. 'Home sweet home. Well, yours anyway.'

'Thanks again, Dad.'

'No problem son, as long as you're okay.'

Scott knew that his dad would watch him walk to his apartment door before waving and driving off. Maybe that's what people did, watched to see if you got through the door safely. Considering what had happened, it made sense for his dad to think this way about him, but there was a nervous hesitancy about it that Scott found disturbing.

-7-

Scott closed the door to his apartment and paused, unsure where to put his keys. He spied an empty terracotta flowerpot and tossed them in.

He found and pressed play on the Sonis – E.L.O's *Strange Magic* started playing in the background.

At the same time, his mobile rang.

'Hi er... Mum, er, yeah he just dropped me off. We ended up grabbing fish and chips... okay, well, he should be with you soon. Alright... will do... bye.'

Scott removed his jacket and dropped it down on the sofa beside Annie, who sat in front of a canvas resting on a cushion.

On her left was a collection of brushes and tubes of paint. An old dinner plate was being used as a makeshift palette. Her jeans and *Marvel* Comics t-shirt were covered with dried splotches.

She lifted her brush at Scott as he sat beside her.

'How is she?' she asked.

'Worried,' Scott replied.

'Should she be?'

Scott shrugged. 'I think she's always been a worrier and no, she shouldn't be – what are you painting – let me see.'

'It's not finished yet.' Annie turned the canvas around.

Scot raised an eyebrow. 'Strange figures standing around in the rain? That's a cheery painting.'

Annie waved a paintbrush around in the air as if conducting a string quartet. 'It just came to me. I like it. It's dreamy.' She turned the canvas back around.

'It's still just dudes standing in the rain, but it's not bad.' Scott smirked.

Annie beamed at him. 'So then, this old woman... the strange nightclub cleaner, have we a new best friend?'

'Hell no! She's a crazy old woman wittering on about missing people and the cold – and wait – when did I tell you about the cleaner?'

'It was the first thing you told me when you walked in. Don't you remember?'

'Did I?'

'There goes the old memory again,' Annie sang.

'Not funny.'

'So – she a crazy old bat?'

'Erm... Full on Mad Hatter's tea party.'

'Perhaps not so crazy Scotty, she does know what you are.'

'And what exactly am *I*, Annie?'

She leaned forward, put the paintbrush in the corner of her mouth and raised an eyebrow.

He rolled his eyes at her, 'Oh, Christ, just leave it? You make me out to be some freak.'

She dropped her shoulders. 'If you wanted women in your life that would roll over and give in, you should have gone for... what was her name, Lucy Simmons, back in the sixth form.'

'I almost did.'

'Really?'

'No, joking.'

'Seriously though Scott, there's more at stake here than just you. What that old woman said today, I don't think it was the ramblings of a psychotic woman. You felt the truth when she spoke to you, didn't you? You're grumpy because you know what she said is true.'

'I'm not grumpy! Why me anyway? Why bloody me?'

'I'm sure nearly all people on their way to becoming something amazing feel the same way and probably think the same thoughts. Perhaps you need to find out for yourself. Maybe... maybe this crazy old woman can help you.'

'How d'you mean?'

'You're a smart cookie. You always had the brains, so listen to her. If she's mad, you can spend the whole time thereafter telling me I told you so.'

'You do realise how tempting that is, don't you?'

They paused and then gave each other smiles.

Annie put her brush down.

'If there is one thing you are not, Scott Finn... it's a freak.'

'I need a coffee.' Scott rose from the sofa. 'Don't suppose there's any point asking you if you want one.'

'You know me so well,' Annie replied handing Scott the painting.

'I don't know you at all,' Scott whispered.

He looked at the canvas in his hand.

It was blank.

He closed his eyes, he could feel it.

She was gone.

-8-

It was a little after 8 am. Squeaking wheels announced Rosemary's presence on the second floor of Euphoria. She ponderously pushed open the door to the ladies' restroom. Checking she was alone, she retrieved her radio from underneath the blue towel refills. She switched it on.

Pharrell William's *Happy* blasted out.

She smiled at the memory of how excited she had been to build an EMF radio. She did not need it now, of course, but there was something old school about it. It was like a comfortable friend in many ways.

She altered the dial and moved towards the cubicle at the end finding her shoes hitting and splashing through water.

'Bloody pipes,' she muttered and turned her attention back to the radio. The music faded, replaced with an imperceptible crackling, and hissing. The interference was getting stronger. She paused and swiped the radio high in the air around the cubicle door finally, holding it at the wall and ceiling. Her mouth fell open.

'Oh no, that's not good,' she muttered to herself. She closed her eyes and lightly pressed her palm against the cool uneven surface of the cubicle door.

'What are you? What do you want?' She didn't expect an answer. She trembled, beads of sweat dotted her forehead and she realised her palms had been pressed upon the cubicle door for a while now. Her muscles burned like fire. Her back and shoulders ached as did her legs, and her stomach gurgled painfully.

'A tree – no, a forest – red – a red forest? Why are you showing me a forest?'

The radio in her one hand wailed out a hideous long whine.

Some unseen force thrust Rosemary back. She fell hard against the row of sinks and slid down; the breath knocked from her body. Her radio clattered to the ground. It lay silent and broken on the floor beside her as darkness crept over her vision.

-9-

Dan Blane was a slim, handsome young man, clean-shaven with tousled hair. He wore designer jeans and a black T-shirt with the words 'Pharaoh-Music' sprayed across his chest in silver. He had been the assistant manager, barman and DJ at Euphoria for over two years which said everything about him. Growing up on the outskirts of the city, Dan had never ventured far compared to his friends. Men in the club were eager to befriend him, while women found themselves captivated by his sexual charisma.

At the sound of the doorbell, he left the cloakroom, whistling as he went and approached the front door of the club. He searched through a huge bunch of keys.

The doorbell rang again.

'Okay, okay. Just a minute!'

He pulled open the heavy door. In front of him stood a man with facial stubble and dark chin-length hair pulled back, secured into a half-bun. He looked like a Viking.

'Morning,' the man said. He seemed distracted, staring at the words on Dan's T-shirt.

Dan raised an eyebrow.

'Erm— yeah sorry, I'm Scott from Finn Plumbing. I'm here to start a job. Maria Gilbert arranged it.'

'Oh, yeah, sweet. I'm Dan. Yeah, Maria, she's the manager, she told me you were coming. Early bird, eh? Come in... you want a hand with your...' Dan pointed to Scott's empty hands, 'stuff?'

'Nah,' Scott grinned, 'I'm okay. I parked around the back again by the escape doors.'

'Yeah, sweet. I'll open them for ya.'

Dan stood aside gesturing for Scott to come through. 'We got a lot going on here at the moment. The place is falling apart but I guess you know all about building regulations.'

'Busy day then?'

'Yeah. Busy, busy, busy. If you can sign in just here,' Dan slapped his palm down on an open diary, 'I'll take you up to the fire door.'

'Your T-shirt, the name Phaedrus Music, where have I heard it before?' Scott asked.

'You mean Pharaoh Music, it's an independent British record label. Are you into electronic music?'

'I'm not sure, I sort of like a bit of everything but the name kinda rang a bell with me so I must have seen it someplace,' Scott replied.

'Sweet.'

Dan saw the plumber narrow his eyes and look around. 'Been clubbing here before? You look familiar?'

'No, I don't think so.'

Dan greeted other staff and workmen as they moved along one of the corridors. He indicated the main office to the plumber. They turned a corner, and Dan noticed Scott slow down and glance at the base of the wall. Then he stopped and looked down at the carpet.

Dan raised an eyebrow but continued walking. He opened the fire doors at the end of the hallway and stood staring across at Scott's van.

'What's up with her?' He heard Scott ask from behind. Scott caught up and walked through the door and into the sunlight, 'Rough night?'

'Eh?

Scott laughed. 'That woman.'

'Woman?'

'The woman in the corridor back there looks like she hasn't been home yet. Is she all right? Looks in a bit of a state.'

'What you on about mate?' Dan frowned, 'What woman?'

He studied the plumber's face. It showed total bewilderment at the question. The plumber stepped back and pointed down the hall.

'That one there?'

The corridor was empty.

'Where? Must be one of the bar staff or something mate,' replied Dan turning away thinking he had a possible nutter on his hands. He stepped through the escape doors wanting to quickly change the conversation. 'Hey, I've seen your van around before... yeah, Finn's Plumbing that's the name.'

'All Finn's bright and beautiful, all plumbing great and small. I work everywhere,' he heard Scott say cheerily. 'Yeah, you'll have seen me around.'

'Catchy branding. No, wait! Do you ever go to the dog rescue centre by Acre's near the scrap yard? The one on Cross Mount? I swear I saw it there not long ago.'

The plumber nodded. 'Er, yeah you would have. I donate dog food there or I think I used to... or so I'm told. A family ritual kinda thing. My mom always buys an extra bag of treats or dog food.'

The plumber looked uncomfortable.

'Sweet! My sister would love you.' Dan folded his arms. 'She loves dogs. What dog have you got?

'I don't think... I mean, I don't know if I ever... shall I move my van or is it okay there?'

'Oh, yeah, shit, sorry man. If you can just back it up to the other side over there by the bins so that the other guys can get in with their gear later, that'll be sweet.'

'Will do,' Scott said and headed to his van.

'Meet you back in the office and we'll sort the paperwork out. Get a coffee and you can get started,' Dan shouted after him.

The plumber gave Dan the thumbs up and walked away. Dan returned to the corridor shaking his head. Once out of sight, he fidgeted with his hair and glanced around. 'Bloody liar,' he muttered.

***

Scott waited for Dan to walk off.

Quickly, he took a few quick steps back towards the emergency exit. The young woman had gone. She'd been there slumped on the floor at the base of the wall. He was sure of it. Lilac vest and jeans her clothes wet, her face beaded and streaked with tears. She'd held a hairbrush tightly in her right hand. She had been real, she had to be.

He raced down the corridor opening door after door, all unlocked.

Didn't anyone care about security?

He shoved open the doors of a storage cupboard, restroom, an electrical meter room, a tiny style-smelling office, nothing.

***

With ladders and a toolbox in hand, Scott walked across the dance floor. He stopped and had a quick chat with two electricians working on a lighting rig.

Walking through the corridor, he glanced down at the spot where he had seen the girl slumped on the floor. Something had been familiar about her.

Did he know her? Or was it the situation she was in?

He was sure Annie would know who she was. Annie seemed to know everyone. He was unsure how he knew.

Something else about being in the nightclub ignited a memory. It bothered him. But the more he focused, the more the memory faded. He tensed up. A feeling of uncertainty grew in him together with the realisation that something strange was happening here.

He made his way up the carpeted stairs to the second floor. He paused at a poster advertising 'Phaedrus Music' and recalled Dan's T-Shirt having the same graphic and logo. He had said it was an independent record label but it read 'Phaedrus' not 'Pharaoh' as Dan claimed.

Something was eerily familiar about this name too. Not in the same way as remembering something but more like an intuition.

Scott dismissed the conscious thoughts growing ever larger in his mind and heaving the stepladder up he made his way to the ladies' restroom. He pushed the door open with his foot. It bumped against a cleaning trolley, sending bottles of mirror cleaner and sanitizing spray tumbling. Scott set down his ladder and toolbox and bent to pick up the bottles.

'Sorry!' he called.

Silence.

The cleaning lady lay unmoving on the floor.

-10-

Scott froze for a few seconds.

The elderly cleaning lady groaned and began to stir. She was struggling to get up off the wet floor among pieces of what looked like parts of a smashed radio.

Scott ran to her side. Taking her under the arms.

'Okay! I got you. You're fine, you're fine. Your pinny is all wet though. Smells a bit of beer too!'

'I'll have you know it's a purple premier pocket tabard!' Rosemary snapped, clinging to the plumber. 'And you try to get the smell of beer out on a 30-degree wash.' She struggled to her feet.

'Couldn't you put it on a hotter wash?'

'And risk a faded tabard? Are you mad? My mother would turn in her grave!'

'Well, I see the fall hasn't affected your dazzling personality. What happened? I'll fetch someone. A first aider?'

'I'm fine. I'm fine. Stop fussing, I only slipped,' Rosemary snapped again.

Scott picked up part of the broken radio and flipped it over in his hands.

The woman snatched it and quickly pushed it into the large front pocket of her tabard.

'You're the last face I expected to see and for the record sunshine,' she jabbed a finger at his chest, 'I'm not from a mental home!'

'Wow! You know how to hold a grudge, don't you? Look Mrs, I just want to... well, apologise for yesterday. What happened... the way I acted. I was having a bad day and–'

'Looks as if I'm the one having the shit day today, so that makes us even.' She held her left arm and winced in pain.

Scott gave her a nervous smile, shocked that the word *shit* had come from this woman's mouth.

'Oh, come on, you spouted all that stuff yesterday, what's a bloke supposed to think?'

'Yet here we are again. Did you tell Maria, the club manager about me?'

'No.'

'Thank you. Why not?'

'Why what?'

'Why didn't you tell Maria about me?'

Scott hesitated. 'It was something you said.'

'That you're psychic?'

'No! I'm not... I mean – I don't know. It sounds so stupid out loud,' Scott whispered. 'There's so much going on with – weird stuff and I don't need any of it. I never asked for this.'

The woman smiled and extended her hand.

Scott took her hand warily. As soon as he touched her, his scattered mind settled into calm.

'My name is Rosemary, Rosemary Moon.'

He returned the gesture with a firm response.

'Scott.'

'Okay, Scott. I'll make you a deal. I'll answer any questions you have if you do something for me.'

Scott chuckled nervously. 'Like what? Have you got noisy pipes or a leak at home? I can easily tell you how to–'

'Oh, you're a laugh a minute, aren't you? I need,' she pointed a finger at the aberrant cubicle door, 'information on that cubicle and you can get it for me. That's all! Do it for me and I'll leave you alone.'

'Really?'

'Really.'

'Honestly?'

'I'm always honest. I'll go back to being an eccentric old woman cleaning up vomit and fishing condoms out of toilets. How does that sound?'

Scott rubbed both hands over his face and turned around on the spot. 'You're serious? You're flippin serious! You believe all this psychic crap!'

'Ahem! It's paranormal crap and no, I don't expect you to believe me! Go right ahead and deny the gift, rightly or wrongly bestowed upon you.'

'Wait for a second, you're claiming that things are going on in the world right now that no one knows about? All creatures and sensing spirits? The world isn't like that it—'

'Phooey! Mr Finn, you are here for a reason and I believe something has led you here to this point.' She pointed a finger sharply in his direction.

'And how do you know my surname?'

She rolled her eyes. 'I'm a psychic too, remember? And the question I guess you're going to ask me now is something about... what is life like being psychic... right?'

Scott folded his arms. 'But I don't believe in all that psychic stuff and I didn't tell you, my surname.'

Rosemary pointed to Scott's embroidered name badge on his shirt.

'Oops.'

'Oops indeed. The old ones are always the best.'

'Are you saying I'm some sort of psychic plumber? Oh boy, that just sounds daft.'

Rosemary ignored him and reached into one of her tabard pockets and retrieved a dried reddish brown leaf. She held it between her finger and thumb in front of Scott's face.

'That thing again? What are you going to do with that?' Scott asked.

'I'm not going to do anything. You're going to follow it down the rabbit hole, Alice!'

-11-

Dan came off the phone and looked up as Maria walked in.

She threw her handbag onto the desk. 'What are you doing in my chair?' she asked.

Dan got up and moved. 'Good morning to you too. I thought you weren't in till ten?'

She ignored him and sat down.

'Are the contractors all in?'

'Yup. Electricians not long arrived, and the plumber's already here. We're still down two cleaners. Shaun is doing deliveries and still no word from Gemma. A restroom door in the men's restroom on floor three got kicked in and Rosemary is already here,' Dan replied.

'Another door? What is going on with those cubicle doors?' she stared at Dan blankly before shaking her head. 'Have you got enough of that wood you used?'

'Uh-huh, plenty more where that came from.'

'Good. Now did you contact all the suppliers on the list I gave you and let them know what's going on?'

'Still got a couple of calls to make. Security Plus rang again, I told them you'd give them a call and explain the situation.'

'The situation's simple, Dan. There's no point repairing or updating the existing CCTV or security system with what's going to happen, the directors won't waste the funds,' she snapped.

'The local papers are still calling on the hour, every hour. They seem to know that the police slapped us hard for our lack of security over the whole incident. Have the board of directors mentioned how they want us to handle the press?' Dan asked.

'I'm seeing them this afternoon. They have asked for an update on everything, the police inquiry, repairs and all the rest of it... and no they aren't happy that the local press is all over this missing girl and our so-called inability to have suitable security measures in place to protect young lives.'

'But they're the ones who wouldn't release the funds for the upgrade till the refurb?'

Maria didn't appear impressed. 'Yes, but of course, they won't see it like that despite the million emails to them highlighting our barely adequate systems. These last two years Dan... it's like everything is against me. Why did the missing girl have to be last seen here?'

'Don't you mean missing girls?'

'Yes, Dan! Thank you,' Maria shouted, 'I am aware this isn't the first girl.'

'Uh-huh,' Dan nodded. 'So, any updates from the police?'

'No, not since all the statements were taken. Let's face it they're not going to tell me anything. We're all potential suspects.'

Dan shrugged, 'Sweet, I'll go crack on with the stocktake then I'll finish contacting those suppliers. Then on to repairing that door.'

'Good, I'll go and find Rosemary and a couple of the others. Tell them about the staff meeting later about the you-know-what,' she raised her eyebrows at him with feigned suspicion and stood back up. 'Before I get too settled.'

'It's okay, I'll go get em.' Dan turned to leave.

'No!' Maria snapped. 'You stay here. Get your list of things done. I'll go myself; I need to make sure they're doing their jobs. We've had enough screw-ups here. Anything else goes wrong and I will be booking an exceptionally long holiday.'

***

Scott held out his hand. Rosemary placed a scarlet leaf on his palm.

'You realise, I'm supposed to be working?' Scott said.

'This is your work now. Open your mind and focus on the leaf and only that.'

'The leaf?'
'The leaf.'
'It's a flaming leaf!' said Scott.
'Humour me.'
'Why can't you focus on the bloody leaf?'
'To answer your question, Scott, because I'm not the strongest psychic.

'I feel this leaf is getting a lot of attention for a leaf.'
'It's no ordinary leaf. No ordinary leaf at all.'
'Oh.'
'I'm limited in what I can do. I suspect you're a much higher-level psychic and so better at psychoscopy than me. Now focus!'
'Psycho... what?'
'Psychoscopy, token object reading, now shut up and focus!'
'I don't know what to do.'
'Yes, you do. Stop fighting, just let go and give the leaf your full attention. Imagine you want to study it, know everything about it.'

Scott's brows drew together.

Nothing happened.

His breathing became fast, it reminded him of the way he felt when terrified by nightmares.

Pure white light shone up from his hand bathing his face and his mouth was now wide open; he couldn't move his eyes from the leaf.

Fear rose.

A light breeze filled the room.

The world started to twist and change before him. Turning, he found himself looking across a grass slope to an ancient forest with trees full of scarlet and bronze leaves. Tiny pale flakes danced and meandered down and sailed around the trees like liquid. An endless mass that never appeared to land upon a single blade of grass or branch.

Everything was bathed in an eerie glow that emanated from an empty sunless sky.

Peering harder, farther, he made out a group of tall, hooded figures that stood grouped like a choir. They faced a single figure whose head bowed down. Scott heard voices but couldn't understand.

A figure in the group held up a thin dark hand.

Scott blinked.

The day became night, the sky ominous.

Scott heard screams of frustration and wailing. He desperately scanned between the trees.

'Where are you?' He ran towards the voice.

The darkness appeared to shimmer. Light appeared again. The figures in the distance vanished.

Scott continued running, waiting for a response to his call. He came to a sudden halt and watched as more autumn leaves spiralled in the breeze. He glanced down at one of the leaves now in his palm. An understanding and knowledge filled his mind. He heard his voice, but it was deep with reverberation.

'Blimey... This leaf is... It doesn't belong here.' Struth... do I sound like that? And there's another voice in my head, in the distance. Is that you, Rosemary? This is weird, are you telling me to breathe slowly? Wait! The leaf, I'm getting information about it. It's a maple leaf, Acer Saccharinum.'

'Now, Scott, listen. Just listen to the words you hear in your head. The words that are being whispered to you as you focus on the leaf. Listen and tell me what else they say,' Rosemary instructed.

'Known as Silver maple, Creek... White maple, and hunters, buffalo and eagles... America... no, snow-covered... Canada. This leaf is a species of maple, native to... eastern North America in the United States and Canada. It is one of its most popular trees.'

The pure white light faded from Scott's face. Eyes wide in astonishment, he staggered back.

'What the hell! That was...' he blurted out. 'I could see and hear everything about this leaf. It was like I had it all written in my head! It feels like I've just come off a roller coaster for the first time. That was crazy!'

'How I envy your ability to do that. You didn't even have to try.' Rosemary frowned.

'How d'you mean?'

She lowered her head in concentration. 'Most people, paranormals like us, take a few attempts to obtain some, if any information from an object. You, you just... did it!'

'Is that good? I just had to sort of listen and let go. I could smell the leaf, the tree, the soil it grew in,' Scott said.

Rosemary stepped forward waving her hands across the floor. 'So, the leaves that are appearing from this end cubicle are from a species of tree that originated overseas. But you can find maples here in the UK nowadays.'

'Like in parks and stuff? So, you're saying this leaf hasn't been blown here from Canada?'

'No, no, we have a lot of maples here in our gardens and garden centres. Most are Japanese maples but I'm no Alan Titchmarsh.'

'Who?'

Rosemary put her head to one side and took a careful look at him raising an eyebrow.

Scott stepped forward. 'But no! I mean this leaf here in my hand came from a tree growing in the wild with others, not someone's garden. It was autumn, definitely... yeah, it was autumn. Hold on... I think I've seen these maple trees around. There must be hundreds of varieties and colours.'

'You said you sensed it was autumn but it's April,' said Rosemary.

'This is... messed up,' Scott stammered. 'Hell! What a rush though!'

'You believe me now?' Rosemary asked. She watched him closely. 'Five minutes ago, you couldn't say the word psychic, now you're using it to solve a mystery.'

Scott pointed. 'That doesn't mean I'm going to help you.'

Rosemary paused and wiped her eye. 'Still, think I'm mad? Well, can I ask you some questions like have you been having a lot of difficulties in your life recently?'

'A few, like everyone,' He replied.

'Feel that life is passing you by? Nothing to show for it?'

'Maybe. Why?'

'I'm not sure. It still doesn't explain why you've not displayed any abilities. Some gain their psychic credentials early in childhood, others in their late teens but,' she looked hard at him now. 'This denial, I don't think you fear being a psychic. I believe deep down you're quite excited about it. But something has prevented you from developing your abilities.'

'That's rubbish!' Scott's voice said with a slight exclamation.

'I would hazard a guess that you're afraid you'll lose who you are and that's the reason why you live in the realm of normality. You're scared, you're scared you'll like the new psychic Scott Finn a bit too much. Could I be right?'

Scott placed the leaf on the sink. 'I've already lost who I am so bang goes your theory.' He saw Rosemary's eyes narrow.

'Well, here's the news bulletin, sunshine!' she said. 'You've already stepped out of the stalls. The gun has fired and there's no going back.'

Scott looked back at the door out. 'What if I don't want to? What if I could press reset and reboot myself back to the way I was? What if this isn't for me?'

'It is for you, trust me! I don't know a single person who has regretted– well that's not entirely true, but nearly everyone has loved this life and I believe you will too.'

'How can you know that? You don't even know me!' His voice rose. 'Why couldn't this have happened when I was eighteen or twenty? When it would have been, okay? At least fun. Why now when life's so...' He noticed her frown mirrored in his own expression as he glanced at himself in the mirror. 'Adulthood... adulthood can be messy

Rosemary. It's all... get up, go to work, eat beans, watch television, go to bed, get up, go to work.'

He felt her next to him and together they addressed their reflections.

'All I will say is this. You are not alone in this, Scott, not anymore.'

Scott moved away and spread his arms wide. 'I don't know you. I don't trust you and I don't trust all this. The last thing I need is to be lectured. Everyone telling me what to do – what I should be thinking and feeling – what's going to happen, when and if.'

'Hey, hey, hey. I *do not* expect you to trust me, not yet, maybe not at all and I don't know what's going on in your life, Scott. I feel it's something big but let me say this one thing, please. Take hold of this gift you have and hold it tight. You take it and embrace the adventure that comes with it. Run with it, my boy. You just run! You go and you never look back, never doubt, never regret and never forget.'

'I'm scared okay is that what you wanted to hear? I can't lie, I am scared, I admit it.'

'Do you want to start living? Answer me that and do you want to understand and get some answers?'

'Yes.'

'Then help me. We've only just met and you have little reason to believe anything I say. Trust what you have seen and performed just now with the maple leaf and what you've been experiencing. Please, Scott. I need your help and it may be dangerous but lives, many lives may depend on it.'

-12-

Rosemary looked hard at the last cubicle.

'So,' Scott began, 'what's with the cubicle door then? Are we looking for a direct telephone line from Churchill to Roosevelt?'

'Hmm,' she gave a smile. 'The SIGSALY project secret war telephone in a toilet? Someone knows his history.'

'Wish I did. Not sure how I knew that particular fact!'

'What do you mean?'

'Nothing.'

Rosemary let it go. She moved slowly across the room scanning.

'Over the last thirteen months, four young women have gone missing. All were here at some point the night they disappeared.'

'What are the police doing about it?'

'I don't know exactly. What I do know, however, is that they are under the belief that each woman left this nightclub before they went missing.'

'Maybe that's what happened then. What about cameras, the CCTV? Surely, they saw them walk out with a bloke or with their mates?'

'The cameras were down on two of the occasions,' Rosemary replied. She raised an eyebrow. 'Apparently, no one noticed the recording system's memory was full. It couldn't record anymore. One other recording of the night was too distorted, and a water leak ruined the last batch of cassettes, which conveniently were stored in a waterlogged cellar. One of the reasons you're here, I suppose.'

'Convenient.'

'Very.'

'Witnesses came forward to say they'd seen the women in question leave on all four occasions.'

Scott folded his arms across his chest. 'There you go then, sorted.'

Rosemary laughed. 'Witnesses that had no legitimate connection to any of the missing women, I might add. Not one genuine friend or boyfriend reported seeing them leave.'

'What are you saying Rosemary? These witnesses were... what's the word, bought?'

'I wouldn't rule it out. It's easy enough to sway someone to say they think they saw them leave. It happens a lot more than the public realises. Police understand about the unreliability of eye-witness testimony, but with no other evidence to suggest otherwise...'

'So then, only strangers came forward to say these women left the nightclub premises?' Scott frowned. 'You're talking about four separate incidents, call me stupid but that's a little stretch even for me to believe.'

'Let me illustrate,' Rosemary stopped scanning and gestured toward the last cubicle. 'The final woman to go missing was the Saturday just gone, nineteen-year-old Amy Mansell. Her friend claims that she was standing there, talking to her in this restroom through the cubicle door when she disappeared. But her statement will be taken as a load of codswallop.'

'Why?'

'Because she'll be classed as an unreliable witness due to the alcohol and drugs found in her system.'

'That makes everyone in the club an unreliable witness then. Including those who say they saw them leave.'

Rosemary pointed at him with a smirk. 'Not one of the witnesses had been here in Euphoria allegedly. They were all passers-by who came forward.'

'God, you sound like a late-night detective.'

'We all have a past,' Rosemary said.

'In all seriousness, how do you know they didn't walk out with some guy? Do you know what nightclubs are like? Surely you had them back in your day.'

'Cheeky sod! Anyway, I'm not the strongest psychic, but one thing I can do is something we call residual scanning.'

'Who's we?'

'Too much, too soon, sunshine, I don't want to scare you off.' Rosemary smiled. 'Anyway, a residual scan is the ability to visually view the start and end of someone's physical movement within an environment.'

'Blimey.' Scott screwed his face.

Rosemary huffed. 'Think of it like,' she flapped both hands trying to think and winced at the pain in her arm. 'Like walking through the water as fast as you can. You leave a trail of bubbles, don't you? Or a boat or trawler leaving a trail behind it in the water.'

She stepped toward the last cubicle. 'I was here in this room less than fourteen hours after Amy Mansell came in here. She entered this cubicle and that's where her residual trail ended.'

'You're telling me that you can see the... trail? Like we can follow the smell of cheap perfume?'

Rosemary snapped her fingers. 'Like cheap perfume, exactly.'

'Don't... like... moths have that too?'

'That's more of a vapour trail but similar,' Rosemary said. 'Residual scans are a bit more like... an individual's personal residual echo. I can physically see it as energy as it hangs in the air. If you stick around, you'll get to see it for yourself.'

'A person's residual what?'

'Never mind. Like I said, hopefully, you'll get to see it for yourself.'

'Oh, come on, how do you know it was Amy's trail? There would have been over a hundred women in here Saturday night and then you had the police!'

'You need a sample from the person. A hair, a nail clipping, an item of clothing, something that has their skin cells on it and let's say I was able to acquire some from a friend of Amy's.' She gave Scott a look that said do not ask.

'So what do you need me to do?' asked Scott.

'Just what you did with the leaf, only do it to the door of the cubicle,' Rosemary said, pointing to the last one. 'If you sense nothing then go inside, but any indication of danger then stop. Is that understood?'

Scott nodded. He joined Rosemary in front of the last cubicle door and sucked in his breath. He looked down at Rosemary wide-eyed. 'An indication of danger? What do you mean?'

'Oh, you'll know.' She pushed Scott and regretted it, feeling the stab of pain in her left arm. She gestured, Scott, forward with her good arm hoping she was doing the right thing. She took a step back from him. 'Just focus and most of all... listen.'

'You need to get that arm looked at, a woman of your age,' Scott said.

'Again, very cheeky! I will get it checked after this. Now close your eyes and listen, just listen. If you feel anything that makes you feel bad or sick, then release the door. Let's see what you've got.' She balled her hands into fists and held them at her sides. 'Now... listen.'

-13-

Scott closed his eyes. He could hear dance music pulsing from the ground floor. The bass sent vibrations reverberating through every surface of Euphoria's foundations.

Yet again, it was a sound that was familiar, like old times. Were nightclubs a part of his life before...?

He opened his eyes and shook his head. He knew he had no time for this. What was he doing? Was this honestly happening?

Scott looked carefully at the door of the end cubicle. It was unlike any door he had seen, strikingly different from the others. An amateur had cobbled it together and painted it white or at least attempted to. Now it was discoloured and flaked. Cracks bled down the length of the wood like lightning.

He listened. It was a combination of straining to hear someone and altering your eyes on one of those magic eye pictures he had seen in magazines way back.

Scott felt it first, then he was aware of its presence. It was a moving, flickering shape that appeared at the side of the door. It seemed, at first to be part of the texture of the door itself. Then it appeared to take on a series of quick, broken images.

'There was something here,' he said.

Rosemary took a cautious step forward. 'When?'

'A few hours ago, maybe.'

'An employee? One of the staff?'

'No... I don't think so. It's strange... wait. It's as if whatever it was... was here, but in the wrong sort of way... in a different sort of way.'

'A manifestation?'

'I don't know what that is,' Scott said.

'Something human-like, a recognisable figure but not quite right, not whole,' Rosemary said.

'No, it's more than that, stronger than that.'

'Is there something you can liken it to?' Rosemary asked her voice strict and confident.

'No, because I have no reference for it.'

Rosemary watched as Scott breathed out deeply and slackened his body.

'I can't believe I'm talking like this,' he said.

'We call it your authentic self,' Rosemary explained, 'and you're doing fine son, just fine. Now tell me about the door?'

Scott placed both of his palms against the cubicle door. Pure white light bathed his face and he immediately stood to his full height. His back straight. When he spoke, his voice once again had changed. He was confident, business-like, and coldly efficient. Stolid and controlled.

'Wood, old wood, different from the others here,' he said.

'What type of wood? Can you tell? Narrow it down?'

'Yes... it is maple saccharinum, both the door and the frame.'

'Same as the leaf?'

'Yes.'

Rosemary turned away covering her face. She sighed, 'It's an anchor point! How could I have not known that? I'm a stupid... stupid old woman.'

'I don't understand, this wood is old... I mean incredibly old,' Scott said.

'It's a rift Scott, kept open by a substance or material. Something found at the point of origin and– Wait, wait! Scott, can you sense any women? Try and listen for any of the women.'

'I need names, Rosemary, or an item to attach to.'

'How did you know that you need an item to attach to?'

'Names Rosemary I need them now!'

Rosemary quickly rummaged through her pockets for a particular piece of paper.

'Here, here – Abbi Price, Nadine Bladon, Julie O'Yang, Amy Mansell.

Scott remained silent as he processed the information.

'The bridge opens at intervals. It allows people to pass through and leaves of the maple saccharinum are blown through when they do. The women could have simply walked through... Wait!' He tipped his head to one side. 'Something else...'

'That's enough Scott, step away now.' Rosemary grabbed him by his arm and yanked him back, but he didn't move. Scott's arms remained extended; palms flattened against the door.

'No, wait... It's Amy, I think it's her, it's Amy Mansell.'

'Is she alive? Is she okay?'

'She's lost... I mean she... she's scared, I... Wait... There's something else.'

'That's enough Scott.'

'There's something in there with her.'

There was a blast of icy cold air. Scott flinched as if burned. An eerie blue light began to emanate around the doorframe and flakes appeared floating about the cubicle.

'Scott, back off!' Rosemary urged and grabbed him by the arm again.

'Anger, revenge, shame, anguish, self-disgust,' Scott shouted screwing his eyes shut. 'It sees me, it knows I'm here!'

'Break off, son. Break the connection. Do it now!' Rosemary screamed at him, but he never heard her.

In the silence, Scott opened his eyes.

Fixed to the spot he felt a presence at the side of his head. He strained to move his eyes to the side. A familiar cardboard box began to fill his view. The box was close enough to scrape against his ear.

He leapt back crashing against the sinks. He slid to the ground, chest tight with anxiety, breathing erratic.

An eerie silence swept around the restroom. His gaze fell on the light that shone through a water jug that sat on the sink corner. The same jug from his hospital room in his nightmares. The scent of Estee Lauder filled his senses as light danced on the surface of the cubicle doors.

Then the shadows came.

-14-

Rosemary swore softly as the entrance to the women's restroom flung open. It smashed into the cleaning trolley she had left there on purpose.

Maria walked in glancing first at the trolley and then at her struggling with Scott.

Maria's shoulders dropped. 'What the hell's going on here?'

Rosemary assisted Scott without much success, clearly adopting frail behaviours and trying to hide the pain in her arm.

'I... I don't know. I heard him fall.'

'I'm okay,' Scott said. 'I'm fine, no harm done, ladies.'

'Can you be a little more careful, please? The last thing I need is a bloody health and safety issue on top of everything else. What did you do?' Maria asked.

Rosemary interjected. 'Shall I get you some water, young man?' She knew her act was comical to Scott now by the slight smirk he gave her. She knew he understood it was all part of her performance.

'No, I'm fine,' Scott replied. 'I slipped checking the cistern.'

Maria was now scanning the room. Sighing, she rubbed her hands over her face. 'This place is falling apart. Are you sure you're alright?'

Rosemary saw Scott give Maria a cheeky yet convincing smile.

'Yeah, no problem.'

'Good, so tell me, what's the problem with the cistern and the leaks we're plagued with? Can you at least patch things up to last for– let's say a couple of months?'

Rosemary stepped away and headed to her trolley. 'Why a couple of months?'

Her question was dismissed with the wave of a hand.

'Erm... listen, I've called a staff meeting at twelve. Rosemary, you need to be there... You, er, Scott, is it?'

'Yeah.'

'Staff only. If you can get to me with a rough breakdown of what you need, cost etcetera and pass it on to Dan, that'll make me incredibly happy. If that's at all possible these days.'

'No problem.'

'Rosemary, can you go and make him a cup of tea? Dan's the first aider. I'll send him up just to check you out and fill out an accident report and don't forget, twelve on the lower dance floor.'

Rosemary received a condescending look as Maria marched out of the room.

'Bugger,' Rosemary said, 'I forgot to place a doorway charm at the top of the stairs. It would have turned her away,' Rosemary whispered listening through the door. 'She's gone.'

'You're funny,' Scott said. checking himself over.

'I do try.'

'It works.'

'Now what happened? What did you sense?' Rosemary asked.

'It was there.'

'What was?'

'Ah, nothing.'

'Nothing?'

'Nothing.'

'Scott what? Don't just say nothing! I hate it on television when they do that, it's important, so tell me everything's vital in this job, even the smallest thing.'

She saw how Scott kept his eyes firmly on the cubicle door. 'A person... sort of... that I've been seeing in a few nightmares and stuff.'

'And it was here? With you just now when you were awake?'

'Yeah.'

She continued to watch him as his eyes burned continuously into the door, he looked exhausted and scared.

'What sort of nightmares have you been having, Scott? If anything, your abilities, no matter how delayed or suppressed should be providing the necessary REM sleep. What happened to you, son?'

'Leave it. I know why I'm having nightmares. It's none of your business!' Scott finally broke off his stare and stepped over to his tool bag.

She knew not to push him. 'There's nothing more we can do,' she stated moving over to her trolley. 'Dan will be here in a minute and they'll get suspicious and then this staff meeting. I wonder what that's all about?'

'You mean you don't know?' Scott asked.

'No, do you?'

'Er, well, yeah, Dan told me. It's why I'm here,' He waved a wrench in front of his face. 'Patch the leaking pipes and manage the boiler keep it ticking over till they shut the place down.'

'They're closing the club?'

'Well, for a while anyway from the way he was talking. This part is getting rebuilt.'

'No, that can't happen!'

'It's an old building,' Scott chuckled. 'Rosemary, there are lots of them around. They all need pulling down. They're dangerous.'

Rosemary steadied herself on her trolley.

'Scott, son, you don't understand. I need you to meet me here, tonight, at nine o'clock. Can you do that? And give me your telephone number.'

'What? Why?'

'Because time's up. If you don't meet me, we'll never find those missing women, and this city could be in even more danger than I originally thought possible.'

***

The figure positioned himself low down in a car some distance away from the nightclub. He watched the old cleaner Rosemary leave Euphoria and took note of the time. Then the plumber forty-two minutes later. Those two had been in the restroom on the first floor for a while. He had heard them talking, only catching parts of their conversations. Words like 'tonight' and 'missing women'. It was enough to raise concern.

So near now, so close.

A new plan began to form.

The figure pulled out a phone from his back pocket and tapped on the screen. He would need to call this in and get new orders. They would know exactly what they had to do.

-15-

Betty Sallow sat with a sudden thump and the cups and teaspoons rattled on the pine kitchen table.

'Are you kidding me, Rosemary? Are you telling me a plumber pops up at your undercover cleaning job claiming,' she raised her hands to draw quotes in the air, 'a loss of memory? He may, or may not, be a paranormal like you and he possibly initiates the opening of rifts?'

Rosemary looked up from her teacup. 'He is a paranormal, Betty! I thought you might be more concerned with the missing women and the impact that knocking down that part of the building will have on an already expanding rift.'

'Of course I am, Rosemary. But seriously! Don't you think it's... a little... well convenient that this plumber turns up unexpectedly claiming no knowledge of his abilities?'

'You're right, I can see that it's strange and to be honest, I did think that at first. It's very unusual to find someone as old as he is who hasn't manifested any abilities yet. But the sudden appearance of latent abilities isn't completely unheard of. It's happened before. Maybe it's fate.'

The kitchen door flew open and Carol Moon shuffled in wearing a pair of cartoon cow novelty slippers and wrestling with a basket of laundry. She made an awkward beeline for the washing machine.

'What's happened before?' Carol asked her voice muffled as she used her chin to pin down some unruly bedsheets.

Betty and Rosemary gaped at each other.'

'Erm – ooh – ello luv, I didn't hear you come in. How lo-long have you been here?'

'Bomb bay doors open!' Carol called out ignoring her mother and letting go of the basket which fell to the floor with a bang. 'Not long...'

A startled black cat with a white paw shot from underneath the kitchen table and flew out the backdoor cat flap.

'Bomb bay doors open,' chuckled Betty. 'Military aircraft talk that does take me back to being a girl.'

'...er, that's not our cat.' Carol added eyebrows raised and eyes wide.

'Gittings!' Betty exclaimed turning around to stare at the cat flap. 'That was Gittings!'

'Your cat? Are you sure Betty? It could have been ours?'

'God lord mom! Ozma is light grey and fluffy!' Carol explained.

'I haven't got my specs on,' Rosemary snapped back.

Betty turned back around. 'He must have followed me again, I'm so sorry.'

'Ozma has a boyfriend,' Carol sang getting down to load the washing machine.

'Get rid of her.' Betty mouthed to Rosemary.

Carol rose. 'I'm such a nitwit!' I left the pillowcases on the landing.'

'Oh, luv, can you get my nighty and throw it in the wash as well? It's on my bed.' Rosemary called after Carol as she swiftly left the kitchen.'

'Yeah.' Rosemary heard her call back.

Betty pushed the biscuit tin aside and reached for the pencil and notepad. 'What's his name?' Betty whispered.

'What?'

'What's his name?'

'Who?' replied Rosemary.

'The plumber.'

'The plumber? You mean Scott?'

'Yes, Scott.'

'Scott, Scott Finn, with two n's. What – what are you doing?'

'I'm going to get Jonathan to do a background check. Address?'

'Do you think Carol heard what we were talking about?'

'Well, if she did, she's covering it up pretty well,' Betty answered scribbling Scott's name on the paper.

Rosemary took a sip from her cup. 'I didn't know what to say.'

'Rosemary... the address quickly before she comes back?'

'How would I know his address? Look there isn't any need, I'd know if –'

Betty cut her off midsentence with a swish of the HB pencil. 'You said you sensed a sort of mental barrier, a dark place, like a locked door.' She raised an eyebrow.

Rosemary placed her cup down on its saucer. 'Finn's Plumbing, that's what it said on his work top.'

Betty wrote down the details, folded the paper and put it in her bag. 'Done!'

Rosemary retrieved her handkerchief and wiped her eye. 'Scott may or may not be withholding something which I can't see just yet, everyone has secrets. We have a code of conduct, remember. I can't go grabbing things from his unconscious without permission.'

'Don't be a daft cow! It's not like you're shoplifting a tin of beans at Tesco. Oh struth! She's coming!'

Carol returned holding pillowcases and a lemon floral nighty. 'Is this the one?'

'Oh yes, luv, it's cotton-rich so don't put it on a hot wash.'

Carol looked over at Betty 'She treats me like I've never done any washing before!'

'Don't worry Carol, I used to say the same thing to my two when they were at home.'

Carol finished loading the machine and pressed the 30-degree button. She turned around placing both hands on her hips. 'What are you two talking about anyway? You're acting very odd.'

'No luv, don't be silly we were just talking about when I forgot to pay for my shopping at Tesco.'

'How can I forget you were as mad as a March hare that day like a woman possessed.'

'Maybe she was,' Betty replied winking at Rosemary.

'Fiddlesticks, I was having a senior moment,' Rosemary laughed.

'I'm like that if I drink too much chamomile tea,' Betty chimed in.

Rosemary indicated to the kitchen window. 'I don't think the washing lines up luv and the peg bag is still in the shed.'

'Is that your way of telling me to go do it?'

'Well, I can't do it anymore, I can't push it up, I haven't got the strength.'

Carol rolled her eyes and headed out the back door leaving it wide open.

When the coast was clear Betty leaned forward. 'Look, I need to make tracks in a second but Jonathan and I are normal people – well, I wonder about Jonathan sometimes – but we aren't bound by your paranormal code of conduct. Let Jonathan run a few checks, eh? We've been around you and Henry long enough to know when something smells fishy. You said this Scott has a van with the company name on it. We'll start there.'

Rosemary nodded and glanced up through the kitchen window again. 'I think Carol scared your cat when she dropped the laundry basket.'

'What Gittings? No, he'll be fine. That cat would survive the house collapsing on it. Anyway, stop changing the subject. Jonathan and I can suggest things and research stuff for you, but it's you out there doing it. You're the one who fights the hordes of darkness. As far as we are concerned, you're one of the best. We only wish we could do more. Let us check him out. It'll give me some peace of mind if nothing else.'

'Fine, fine. I used to be so good at this. Where has my instinct gone, Betty?'

'Maybe it ran away with the milkman,' Betty chuckled.

'Blimey, I can't remember the last time I saw an actual milkman.'

'That's settled then,' Betty said getting up. 'I must get going Jonathan's going to wonder where his dinner is.'

Rosemary rose, walked over to the kitchen door and retrieved a coat which she handed to Betty. 'Not the day I thought it was going to be when I woke up this morning. I'll feel a bit better after a little sleep.'

'If we find anything bad, we'll call you, otherwise, we'll leave it and I'll see you Friday. I'll try you on your mobile and if I can't get you on that, I'll ring your house and yes, I'll be discreet because of Carol. Jonathan's going to love investigating. He'll go into detective mode and I won't see him for hours.' She laughed buttoning up her coat.

'Okay.' Rosemary agreed in a whisper. 'You can gather information on Scott and I'll manage the rift but be fast. I can't hold off long on this one. Time is short, I must pass through that rift, find the women and seal it shut somehow. I'll do what I need to do to stop this from happening to more people.'

Betty winked. 'I'll need a custard cream to take with me for the journey.' She walked back over to the table and retrieved the biscuit tin.

'You only live two streets away!'

'I could get lost!'

'Just follow Gittings, he'll take you home.'

Both women chuckled. Betty leaned back in the open door.

'See ya, Carol, luv!'

A few hours later Rosemary heard Carol come down the stairs and into the lounge. Rosemary wrestled with the TV remote.

'I thought you were going to have a lie-down, mom?'

Rosemary blinked over her glasses. 'Hello, luv. No, I couldn't nod off.'

Well, you've missed a first. Your grandson has taken himself off to bed!'

'What! Bed at 5 pm? Well, that's nice, isn't it?' Rosemary replied waving the remote at her daughter. 'It needs new batteries.'

'He's upstairs in his pyjamas looking like a giant Smurf.'

'Oh, he makes a good Smurf.'

'An eight-year-old wanting to go to bed on a weeknight at 5? You don't think he's sick, do you?' Carol asked rummaging through the drawers below the bookshelf.

'I don't think so, luv. I know he's really into that book, Joanne at school gave him, what's it called? Oh, I can't remember.'

Carol passed over two new batteries, then grabbed a handful of clothes off the dining table and began to fold them.

'Mom? When I was a child... did I go up to bed okay or was I one of those who put up a fight?'

Rosemary ignored her daughter and began to fiddle with the remote's battery cover. 'It's some book about a girl running around with a bow and arrow.'

'I imagine as a child I was fairly good at going up to bed, *up the rickety bridg*e as dad would say. I must have been good because I don't have trouble now,' Carol continued, 'and I love getting up in the morning.'

'All the kids are reading this book apparently, but it may be a bit too advanced for George.'

'Mum!'

'What?'

'I'm asking about my childhood!'

'Well, I'm trying to remember the name of the book Joanne lent George. What was it you wanted to know, luv?'

'Was I good at going up to bed?'

'No! You were bloody awful!' exclaimed Rosemary replacing the batteries and snapping shut the compartment. 'There all done.' She lowered herself onto the settee where she began rummaging through her knitting bag. 'Oh luv, will you put my mobile on charge for me? You know I don't do it properly? I'm going to try and have a lie down again. I'm going out tonight so don't wait up.' Out of the corner of her eye saw Carol halt mid-fold.

Rosemary didn't know whether to be concerned or happy about her own behaviour of late. It was true that Carol had not exactly had the most normal or conventional parenting, especially with Henry and herself being police officers. She knew that Carol's life as a child had been eventful, manic and at times lonely. She and Henry had discussed it at great length. They had wanted to protect Carol from some of the cases they had worked on. Carol had understood this as a child. Keeping the paranormal side of their life secret from her had been an early decision.

'What? Where are you off to now? You've been at work today. Have you eaten anything yet, Mum? They're working you too hard at that bloody place. I don't like it.'

'I had a biscuit with Betty earlier. Tonight, I'm only meeting a few friends from the bowling club. It's a birthday drink and there will be food I imagine. I'll just go on up now and pop my head into George's room and kiss him goodnight.'

'Good lord Mom! You're worse than a teenager. Sneaking out, coming back at all hours. It's just like how you and dad used to be. I often wonder lately who the parent is in this relationship!'

Rosemary heaved herself up and walked over to her daughter, took her by the arm and looked into her eyes.

'You turned out a good un, gal.'

'Are you sure you're okay, Mom?'

Rosemary looked away. 'Yes, of course. You'll be alright won't you, luv? You know when my time comes?'

'Mom, stop it will ya! Don't say things like that. You know it upsets me.'

'I'm sorry, luv. I don't mean to.'

'You're missing Dad, aren't you?'

'Always do, luv, always will.'

Rosemary squeezed Carol's arm and trod wearily upstairs.

She popped her head through the door. George was sitting up in bed reading. He had grown up so fast. It was only last year that a seven-year-old had pleaded with her for one more adventure story before lights out. Now, here he was a year older reading on his own. Having George around was one of the positive things in her life. He was his own little person now; someone she could have a conversation with. He had introduced her to new television programmes and computer games, and he was genuinely interested in talking about the old days.

Rosemary gently closed the door. Back in her room lying on her bed, she wondered... would she ever see her daughter and grandson again after tonight.

-16-

Scott stared out of his bedroom window, his breath fogging the surface.

'Annie, you said to me that I couldn't go back to the way I was. So much happened today with this Rosemary woman at the nightclub. Is that what you meant?'

Annie appeared from behind him throwing her arms around him. She hugged him tightly.

'No, not entirely,' she mumbled, 'You're different from the person who left this morning. You've begun to see what you can do. Why would you want to go back to being plain old Scotty-pie? And besides, you can't go back to the man you were before the incident.'

'Why can't I? And why can't I still remember who I was? You're the only person that I recognise in some way, but I still don't know who you are either.'

'Yes, but then I don't think you ever really knew me,' she jabbed him in the side jokingly. 'Not the *me* that stands here with you now.'

'Were you ill, Annie? It's as if I know you were ill or there was something wrong?'

'I was ill, yes, but I'm better now.'

'Let's not talk about it.'

'I said you were going to be special,' Annie said, 'didn't I?'

'I don't feel special.'

'Special enough that this Rosemary woman needs you to save those women tonight.'

'Hell, that sounds so stupid, like I'm on a superhero show. I don't know what she means or if any of it is true, but she was freaked out. I mean really freaked out. Even if she is crazy, I can't ignore what happened to me and if I don't go, she'll be there tonight on her own. The club's not open Tuesdays and Wednesdays.'

'So, do you trust this Rosemary?' Annie asked.

'Yes, I think I do.'

'How do you know you can?'

Scott shrugged. 'I just do. It's like a voice is telling me. I understand that it's part of what I can do. I want to do this. I know I must do it. This morning you were telling me to listen to her. I did and now everything's changed.'

'I know Scotty.'

'And maybe... maybe this will help me remember at least something about my past.'

'I hope it won't,' whispered Annie.

'Eh?' Scott tensed and turned around, but Annie was gone.

He fell onto the bed and closed his eyes.

He dreamed.

The ceiling fan rotated gently on the ceiling of the hospital room. The window blinds were now closed. The water jug sat on the cabinet with a plastic beaker and the smell of Estee Lauder hung in the air.

Scott listened for the nurse. He heard nothing. He sat up and looked left. On the wall, a framed picture showed a weathered wooden post with three signs giving directions: *Coastal path... Mortehoe 1.2 miles.... Morte Pointe 0.5 miles.* In the background, the sky was clear and gravestones looked out over a cliff towards the sea.

A faint white light appeared, moving down the wall like a zip unfastening slicing through the picture. It pulsed slowly, getting stronger and stronger until a blue glow emerged at the edges of the white light. The whole room shone.

The water jug once more cast shards of dancing light over the adjacent walls.

Scott slipped off the bed and walked into the light.

***

Rosemary opened her eyes and looked at the clock. It was almost time to go.

She gathered her EMF radio making repairs as best she could. Most of the damage was superficial. A bent antenna, a cracked plastic frequency display and the handle which she used to hold the device away from her body to avoid bioelectricity.

Finally, she finished. It would have to do. She stuffed it into a cloth bag along with her purse.

With a deep breath and a smile, she turned and looked at her reflection in the dresser mirror.

Her smile faded.

'You are one stupid bloody old woman, Rosemary Moon. What the hell are you playing at? They were right. You're too old for this.'

With a final glance at Henry's picture, she walked downstairs, took her coat, and went out into the cold night air.

-17-

Scott pulled up in front of closed factory gates, a couple of streets away from Euphoria. He got out of his van and fastened his green military-style jacket. The sounds of a busy city could be heard a short distance away.

Scott looked back along the road. He huffed a laugh. Wasn't this stupid, here he was creeping around the city at night as if he was in an episode of *Most Haunted*... and yet excitement bubbled in his chest.

He glanced at his watch and headed across and down the side street that led to the club.

An ominous silence hung over the street despite being in a city. Surprisingly clear of debris, Scott thought as he spied two CCTV cameras attached high to the walls above Euphoria's entrance. The neon sign hummed.

He did not have long to wait.

Rosemary appeared from the shadows wiping her eye with a handkerchief. She carried a cloth bag and a bunch of keys.

'Thanks for coming.' Her voice sounded flat and emotionless.

Scott watched as Rosemary opened the reinforced black doors and waved her fingers at the security system on the wall.

'That's odd,' she said.

'What's that?'

'The alarm system is already off, deactivated.'

'I thought you said no one was here?' Scott whispered walking through the doors.

Rosemary ignored him.

Her eyes were closed. She turned her head to the side and her left hand began to reach out.

Scott watched listening to his breathing.

'There is no one here, not in this building anyway,' Rosemary said at last. 'It's just us.'

'Really?' Scott whispered again.

'Really and stop whispering.'

'Why do I get the feeling you've done this before, Miss Marple?'

'We all have a past, sunshine. Maybe if we get through all this, I'll tell you about it.'

'So, you keep saying, but you're... you're a cleaner at a nightclub.'

Rosemary rolled her eyes at him and closed the front doors behind them.

***

Shrouded in a doorway opposite Euphoria, he watched as the man with Viking hair wearing a green military jacket and the old white-haired woman with a handkerchief entered the club. He emerged from the darkness and darted to the double front doors of the nightclub.

From a backpack, he pulled out a padlock and chain and carefully wove it between the door handles. Finished, he slipped the backpack on and padded to the end of the building, where a narrow gated passage separated the club from the warehouse next door.

He got out his phone and began tapping on the screen.

-18-

Scott watched as Rosemary opened a small cupboard door in reception and flicked on a few light switches.

Cold silence.

The smell of beer and damp carpets hung heavier than before.

It was sad to see everything switched off as if the building were holding its breath, lacking life and energy. Clubs were always so vibrant and alive. Scott seemed to know that, seemed to understand that at a deeper level. Images flashed through his mind; images he felt he needed to forget.

Rosemary pushed past jolting him back to the present. He followed as she entered the lower bar and dance floor.

'You don't honestly believe that's what I am?' she called back.

'What?'

'A flaming cleaner?' said Rosemary.

'Well, aren't you?'

'Well... no, of course not. I'm only here as a cleaner to investigate the disappearances. As soon as I got a whiff that something paranormal was going on, I got a job here. I needed to be on site. What do you expect me to be? A DJ? Exotic dancer?'

'So, what are you then?'

'Retired!' she winked at him. 'Come on, we have to get to that bloody cubicle, pardon my French.'

***

The figure outside returned his phone to his jeans, unzipped his coat and retrieved a heavy key from an inside pocket.

He unlocked the gate.

The squeal of metal hinges made him glance up and down the empty street before passing through and into the shadows between the buildings.

He trod carefully over debris, plastic bags, chip papers, bottles and things he'd rather not mention, right through to the rear of the warehouse. It opened into an unlit concrete yard.

Despite the darkness, he navigated around vans and bins confidently. He climbed onto a set of wooden pallets set against the wall and leapt over. He landed between large metal industrial bins in the backyard of Euphoria.

The backdoor to Euphoria's kitchen had a small window from which the electric flycatcher cast a blue light illuminating the yard.

He strode passed the bottle bins and a couple of padlocked outhouses before launching himself up the fire escape.

At the top, he paused and stared out across the city, rain was in the air.

Turning to the fire door, he gently removed a tiny piece of cardboard from between the door lock and its frame.

The door opened with a click.

He held his breath and waited a few seconds.

He had turned the alarms off but it still made him nervous.

He pushed the door open a little more, scanned the dark interior and passed through leaving the door slightly ajar.

Minutes later, the backdoor to the kitchen opened, flooding the area with more blue light. He stepped out and padded over to one of the outbuildings. He unlocked the padlock and swung open the heavy wooden door.

There was an eerie silence inside.

He tapped his phone and swept torchlight ahead of him. He moved around giant white laundry bags tied up, ready for collection in the morning.

He would be long gone by then.

He approached the back of the storage room.

Reaching, he pulled off a large dust sheet used for protecting the technical equipment.

Underneath, lay an unconscious girl with dark skin, curled into a semi-foetal position. He was familiar with her name: Jax.

The figure smiled.

***

The restroom lights flickered on with a gentle hum as Rosemary and Scott walked in.

Cautiously, they walked down the row of cubicles and stopped halfway.

It seemed the nearer they got to the last cubicle the more spooked Scott became.

The being with the cardboard box covering its head haunted him. Not only in his nightmares but now when he was awake. Scott closed his eyes for a moment as if he could somehow blot out what he remembered. Why had Rosemary not pressed him about this strange being?'

'We're going to go through, Scott.'

He opened his eyes, 'Through where? And are you going to tell me why?'

Rosemary looked at him.

He could see that she was struggling to trust him and who could blame her, they'd only just met.

She turned away.

'Over the last year, this gateway... this rift, has been getting larger. It's opening more times now than ever.'

Scott's breath caught in his throat, 'Why would it do that?'

'We can rule out the natural formation of a rift because you sensed Amy and someone else on the other side. Maybe, whatever or whoever it is, created the rift because it wants passage through.'

'So, let's just close it off. If it's a ruptured pipe, then you seal it off. Find the stop cock. They're knocking down this part of the club anyway. Hey, presto! No rift, no gateway, right? It'll do the job for us.'

'Not when the rift is energy ripping a hole in the membrane of reality. If they do go ahead and knock this part of the club down then they open the rift further,' explained Rosemary. 'This rift will become the size... of whatever replaces it. And it'll keep expanding, or to use a metaphor you're familiar with, it'll flood the place.'

'Hell!' Scott said.

'Literally, and we will have no way to stop it or find the young women, and I'm not losing the women.'

'Sounds like you've seen this type of thing before?'

Romary frowned. 'Similar, but not the same. It's never the bloody same. We learn that early on in this business.'

'Who's we?' Scott asked.

Rosemary ignored him and turned away. She retrieved the radio device from her bag and switched it on. 'Come on, old girl, don't let me down.'

An eerie static sound filled the room.

Scott looked at the device and glanced at Rosemary who smiled looking from the radio and then back to him.

He recognised the radio from the parts scattered on the floor after she had collapsed. It was now held together with pale masking tape.

'A temporary botch-up job,' she said. 'It's a radio combined with an EMF machine. Let me turn it up.'

Blue light faintly emanated from under the cubicle door.

'Wow! You don't waste any time?' Scott stepped back. 'That was quick! Nice gadget.'

'That wasn't me,' explained Rosemary. 'The EMF radio isn't even pitched correctly yet.'

Scott shuddered, zipping his jacket.

'Falling temperatures are normal, Scott. I've just never seen it happen so quickly. It's as if...' she turned directly to him. 'It's like we're being invited, which means once we pass through there must be some method of opening the rift and returning. Let's hope so anyway.'

Something, some inner voice, urged Scott to leave, run away, hide. But it was as if he had felt this way many times before. It was almost all too familiar and he knew it had little permanence.

Rosemary took the few remaining steps to the cubicle at the end. Stretching forward, she pushed open the door using the radio.

Blue light shone out and scarlet leaves whisked through and up into the air around her. Scott stood mesmerised as the leaves came to settle about them.

'I'm terrified, I don't care if you know that,' he said.

'Me too, luv, me too. Think of the ones you love, the ones we're saving,' Rosemary said.

'But how? How are we going to save them and stop all this? No guns, no weapons of any kind, nothing. We don't even know what's through there!'

'True, but there's no one else. I already asked around and made the calls. I asked some people – some people I know – weeks ago. Noah at the Green Street ghost group. I used to be on their committee. He's a paranormal too but still overseas. Let's just say the rest of the group won't be helping us anytime soon. They turned their back on me. London hasn't answered my calls or returned my messages either. So for now, it's you and me.'

Scott smirked. 'You seriously belong to a ghost group?'

'Don't underestimate the whole notion of ghost hunting. They are usually one of the first places people go to for help. These groups are more open to the paranormal phenomena than the regular authorities will ever be.'

Scott rubbed the back of his neck. 'But seriously, a ghost group?'

'I've ended up with a lot of cases from these groups over the years.'

'Is that how you found out about this place?'

'No,' Rosemary replied. 'One of the capabilities of all paranormals is being able to feel paranormal phenomenon. Some of us are extremely sensitive, others not so much but we can all do it. The only drawback is that we need to be close to the anomaly.'

'And why do you think your friends haven't got back to you?' asked Scott.

'I don't know. It can't be anything good.' She raised a finger and gave a playful smile. 'Or they could just still be upset with me.'

Scott looked back to the exit door hoping to see someone walk in. Someone who would talk him out of what he was about to do. If Rosemary was right then everyone he had loved, that he had cared about, would be gone, lost to something mysterious.

He shrugged, everyone he had ever loved, that was hilarious. He did not remember anyone; let alone anyone he had emotions for. However, a new unfamiliar sensation suddenly overwhelmed him. An understanding that took moments for his brain to compute.

He wasn't scared anymore.

He felt no fear.

He had no idea who he was when he woke up on that day back in February or what had happened to him. He had not recognised the name 'Scott Finn' when four days later he was identified. He had not known the two individuals who sat at his side in the hospital bed claiming to be his parents. They had raised him, but they were strangers. They said they loved him but he didn't know them.

The doctor said it was not the typical memory loss that he suffered from. Granted, he was unaware of certain events that had transpired. He had forgotten basic known histories such as two world wars, the death of Princess Diana, and the Twin Towers falling. Yet he could recall with ease cultural references and quotes.

But right here, right now, he was not scared anymore. He had no fear. Only the inexplicable desire to find the answers to so many questions.

He watched Rosemary place the EMF radio beside her bag on the sink before stepping into the cubicle and vanishing amidst the ethereal blue glow.

'I can handle this, I can handle this,' Scott said. Without hesitation, he strode in after her.

***

Rosemary's phone rang out for the third time in a matter of minutes. Carol Moon picked it up, unplugged the charger, and flipped it over to read the screen: Betty Sallow, 3 missed calls.

'Mom, you'd forget your head one of these days.' She placed the phone down and left the lounge. She was heading upstairs when the house phone rang again. Carol huffed four steps up, paused and returned down to the hall and picked up the receiver.'

'Hello'

'Hello, Carol? It's Betty. Is your mum there?'

'No, she's out, meeting some people from the social club, bowling I think she said. Aren't you with her?'

'No not tonight, Carol, chick, got other things to do. I've tried to call your mom on her mobile.'

'Yes, she went out without it again. It's been here charging. Can I give her a message?'

'Oh lord!

'Is something wrong Betty?'

'Oh, oh no, chick I have to speak with her as soon as possible, that's all. If you hear from her, can you pass on the message that the plumber isn't good and not to bother and to call me immediately, she will understand.'

'What's mum up to now? Flirting with a plumber?' Carol laughed.

'No dear, it... it's the social club, just a few problems. Trying to get sorted, you know what your mum's like. Now don't forget, will you?'

'No Betty, I'm trying to find a pen that writes, oh sod it! I'll remember to tell her anyway Betty.'

'Good I'll... I'll speak to you soon, Carol. Bye.'

'Bye Betty.'

Carol replaced the receiver.

-19-

It was the doctors who had called it the incident.

Scott was sitting on a grassy bank, looking over a caravan site. An ornate blue iridescent glass bottle in one hand and a half bottle of beer in the other. The sky was overcast, dry but cold and he had some idea that it was late winter. A small stream trickled behind him.

He looked at the bottles in his hands and placed them both on the grass.

He jumped as children squealed nearby. They were playing games weaving throughout the caravans. Music came from one of the nearby vans, but he did not recognise the tune.

Confusion swept over him as he sat there staring at a scene he had never before witnessed. He did not know where this place was.

Turning around he saw a pub sign. It advertised homemade steak and ale pie, chips and peas. He heard cars on a distant road and sparrows chatting in the hedges.

He kept waiting, hoping that his mind would clear. It was some temporary blackout, it must be. Aside from not knowing where he was, he realised that he did not know 'who' he was.

What was his name?

How old was he?

Why was he here?

The more he tried to remember the more quickly he breathed and the more his heart pounded.

Was he ill?

He put his hands up to examine them. His nails were bitten away and the skin at the sides was swollen and sore. He checked his body. All seemed in working order.

He went through the pockets of the clothes he wore and found nothing, not a single thing, not even a phone or a piece of gum. His trainers were smudged, worn and dirty and his feet hurt. Why were his feet aching, had he walked for hours? And why was his head throbbing so much? He must have hit his head. Yeah, that must be it, he thought. It was obvious, it was the only thing to explain it. That must be it. He had hit his head and passed out.

He viewed everything around him, not with horror, but with a new sense of urgency. His eyes darted as if he needed to assimilate everything his visual cortex could process.

A young couple with an enthusiastic red spaniel walked past and stared at him.

Why were they staring at him?

What should he ask them?

He wanted to hide, run away but something deep inside would not let him.

He stood and followed the couple as they walked by the stream. Eventually, they climbed worn weathered stone steps up onto a bridge that appeared to mark the beginnings of a small high street.

He wondered how he would ask someone about who he was, and would they even believe him?

He stopped an elderly gentleman on the path and laughingly told him that he had no idea who he was, and could the gentleman help him. The man kept walking dismissing him, his expression showing fear.

It was impossible to know where he was. There were no signs that he could see.

He carried on down the high street past more people but was too afraid now to ask them.

The sight of a red telephone box made him pause. He felt calmer peering at it. It was like he knew it. He imagined it was like seeing someone familiar.

As he examined it, wondering why it fascinated him so much, a young woman came out of a nail shop and collided with him.

'Sorry!' they both said simultaneously. He looked at her. She seemed kind. 'Could you tell me where I am? I think I'm lost.'

He disliked the way the woman's face suddenly changed. She took a step back.

'I think I've lost my memory,' he continued.

The woman clutched at her handbag and pointed further down the high street.

'The cottage hospital is down there on the right, next to the chemist.' Avoiding eye contact, she forced a smile and quickly hurried away.

He walked in the direction the young woman had pointed. He was now aware of how others in the small high street were staring at him and acting fearful.

Shaking and starting to feel cold, he stayed close to the shop fronts.

A bar called The Black Horse, a flower shop where three women chatted and laughed. The smell of eggs, bacon and toast came down a small alley to his right and made him feel sick. A barber's shop made him stop for a moment. Glancing through the steamed-up window, he wondered, when was the last time I had a haircut? What was his hair like?

He continued walking.

As he went, he caught distorted reflections in shops and car windows of a figure he did not recognise. An oversized grey sports-style jacket covering a discoloured white shirt. Dark chin-length unkempt hair. His complexion was more a bronze colour giving him a flushed appearance which to some may have signalled that he was healthy if not for the dark rings around his lifeless and empty eyes.

Finally, he stood at the base of the stone stairs leading up to the small red-brick hospital.

Was this real?

Was it a nightmare or some practical joke?

Was it a television show, or was it a film where the characters could wipe memories after questioning potential witnesses? He clearly remembered one.

He wrapped his arms around himself as he considered the huge doors that marked the entrance to the hospital.

He was conflicted, feeling stupid but at the same time embarrassed because of his predicament. He looked to his left at Millie's Grocers shop. He could name all the fruit and vegetables neatly lined up outside in front of the shop window. Next to that, 'Phaedrus Café' had signs in the windows advertising types of coffee that were familiar to him. So why could he not recall who he was?

Before he walked up the steps to the hospital door, some instinct made him turn around.

He spied an older man with sandy blond hair some distance down the high street dressed in a buff dress suit staring right at him.

In a moment of hope, he thought the man must recognise him. Then he realised that the man could just be watching the entrance to the cottage hospital.

Holding his hands tightly together, he walked up the stairs and through the sliding doors.

-20-

Rosemary opened her eyes. The grassy ridge below her feet gave way to a vast forest. Thousands of trees cloaked with scarlet leaves swept majestically away as far as the eye could see. She spied clearings at regular intervals. In these, she was unable to see the forest floor due to a low dense white mist. It hung about the tree trunks like liquid. In some sat large dark triangular-shaped structures like shrines or temples. Giant supports holding the shrines above the ground came into view as the mist swirled and twisted like a living organism. They looked like ships floating on a sea of white clouds.

All through the air floated tiny white crystal-like flakes. Together with scarlet leaves, they danced about, caught up in air currents, lifted high into a warm but ominous grey sky.

Rosemay watched one of the red forked leaves as it fell in front of her and then vanished. Several seconds later another came to rest at her feet.

'My God,' Rosemary whispered as she turned around. Her eyes fell on giant individuated stones that formed a circle of eight monoliths each taller than any man. Each one was both elegant and imposing. Several cardboard boxes lay strewn around. On her right, away from the arrangement was a new different structure, comprising of three huge stones standing six metres in height. These stones supported one flat stone which lay horizontally on top... a dolmen.

Despite the situation she couldn't ignore or deny herself these moments of sheer wonder and majesty. To stand here, to greet another environment that few, if any, had ever seen. This was why she continued to explore. To investigate, to push the boundaries beyond normal life. At a time when all others had told her, enough was enough, finish up, give up, hang up your coat. After experiences like this, how can one be expected to stop? How could she have even let herself think that?

This was who she was. Standing there looking over the forest, she felt young, still with purpose, able to do so much more. She could almost believe she could defeat any evil.

She glanced behind and smiled.

Scott was passed out on the grass, but he was breathing steadily. Cardboard boxes lay scattered around him looking out of place. Being unconscious was a normal response the first time you travelled through a rift... if you were lucky.

Another red forked leaf fell in front of her like the last ones. It felt like autumn.

The first time she'd stepped through a rift was so long ago. February 1979. A lifetime ago! The splitting headache had lasted two days.

Others had reported becoming dizzy and nauseous. And hadn't one woman been adversely affected by the dimensional energy? She's slipped into a coma! Yes, that was right! It was no secret that repeatedly moving through dimensional rifts influenced the mind and non-humans appeared significantly more vulnerable.

Maybe with Scott, she had found a new purpose and an even better reason to stay and fight the good fight.

She took a few steps focussed on the horizon. 'Beautiful!'

Eyes narrowing, she turned her head back to the dolmen. She walked over, a hand raised, fingers spread she swept them slowly over the stone's smooth surface.

'Interesting!'

Returning to Scott's side, she lowered herself down with a sigh and took his hand.

She hesitated.

'I'm sorry, Scott, but I need to know.'

She closed her eyes, reached out and listened.

Rosemary found herself standing in a sun-drenched attic next to a teenager. She recognised him. An unfamiliar second teenager knelt on the floor. His back was to her as he rummaged through a collection of game cartridges next to a console. The room was full of models and action figures. On the walls were posters for *Another 48 Hours* starring Eddie Murphy and Nick Nolte, and another for *Buffy the Vampire Slayer*. *The Prodigy* was blaring from a *JVC* ghetto blaster balanced precariously on top of a radiator.

Rosemary stared down at the figure on her right.

A young man swept his floppy dark fringe out of his eyes and beamed up at her.

She had expected to see an adult Scott but quickly understood why she was seeing him as he was here.

'That's my mate, Darren,' young Scott indicated.

'What is this place, Scott?' Rosemary asked.

'You wanna play on the Sega? Darren's brought it round for us,' Scott said, sidestepping the question. 'I got a PlayStation if you wanna go on that.'

'No, luv, not just yet. Where are we? What is this place?'

'It's the attic at my house.'

'Your attic... you like it here, Scott. You feel safe.'

'Yeah, it's great,' young Scott agreed. 'It's the best place ever! We play for hours, well, at least till mom calls us for dinner or till Darren has to go home.'

'That's lovely, luv, but I need you to take me somewhere further into your future. Take me to when you're older.'

The scene washed away to reveal an untidy, dimly-lit apartment littered with bottles and fast-food containers. A radio in the kitchen sizzled through dance music and voices shrieked in conversation from distant rooms. The strong smell of decayed food and sweat hung in the air like an invisible fog.

Scott... could this be Scott who staggered in before her?

His eyes were bruised with sleeplessness, his face glossy with sweat and empty of emotion. He kicked some clothes onto the floor and fell on the sofa. He pushed his hand under the cushion to retrieve a bottle. It was empty. He threw it to the floor and struggled back up. Digging a full bottle of vodka from the dresser's drawer he returned to the sofa and continued to stare at the wall.

The scene washed away.

In the nightclub, Rosemary couldn't help but observe Scott as he discreetly surveyed the surroundings with a group of similarly dressed men. Amidst them, a young woman with dark hair seemed impervious to his covert manoeuvers. She persistently sought out Scott, engaging him in conversation, determined to coax him onto the already crowed dance floor. Scott merely blew her off, and he and his friends darted off suspiciously into a stairway. Here, they removed tiny hidden plastic bags from shoes and underwear. Each one contained white powder which they carefully tapped out into lines on the backs of their hands. A shortcut straw was eagerly passed around and the powder disappeared.

Rosemary trailed Scott around the nightclub. She watched as he skilfully exchanged cash for small, folded packages. Subsequently, his friends dispersed into a haze of dry ice and bodies. The dark-haired girl appeared again. Scott yelled at her to go away and she fled. At the entrance to the club, a hefty security guard received a squeeze on the forearm and a wad of notes for his cooperation.

Scott left the nightclub.

'I'll take you into the garden,' a voice said.

Rosemary spun to see the teenage Scott again and the scene once more washed away.

Freshly mowed grass and the hum of insects greeted them both. Rosemary and young Scott walked across the lawn of a stately home surrounded by island beds. Each one was filled with mature shrubs and summer flowers, Phlox, Dahlias, Helenium and Dianthus.

'Scott, why are we here? Can you take me back to the time you are avoiding I need to go there. I have to see it.'

'I like it here though,' Scott muttered. 'We always used to come here, look over there. There they are.'

Scott extended his arm, indicating a stunning sun terrace in the distance. On it, four figures stood perfectly still, their gaze fixed intently on them.

Rosemary shivered.

'Who are they, Scott?' She asked.

Scott swept his foot over the grass from side to side before he answered.

'It's only my mom and dad with my big brother, James, and my sister, Jessica. My brother's moving over to America soon. Jessica hates coming here, but mum and dad think she loves it. She'll be leaving soon too for a university in London.

'I don't understand,' Rosemary took a step forward. She raised her arm and squinted in the sunlight to see the family. 'Scott, can you take me back to the months before we met?'

'No!' Scott sounded surprised. 'Why would I want to go back there?'

Rosemary spun round. 'Because I need to know who I'm working with. I want to help you. I need to understand why your abilities were... something is different with you. Forgive me but I need to know that you're on my side.'

'I'm sorry. I can't take you to where you want to go,' Scott said. He huffed and strode off over the lawn heading for a path leading to two enormous Edwardian greenhouses.

'Why not, Scott, why not?' Rosemary called out, following.

Without looking back, Scott's arm gestured to the right. 'Because of that!' Scott shouted back and he ran away.

Rosemary turned in the direction he had indicated. A magnificent ornate arched wooden door held between two stone pillars stood in the centre of the lawn.

It had not been there a moment ago.

It reminded Rosemary of the large doors of a church. They were certainly similar in size. She would not have been surprised to see monks from the Middle Ages filing out.

As she approached, she observed the intricacy of the design carved into both the stonework and the dark aged wood. She reached out towards the structure with her senses. She felt no negative energies and found little to suggest anything was in front of her.

She walked around the structure examining up to the top of the heavy door and back down again.

'I know what you are,' she whispered. 'Over the years I have seen many objects of all shapes and sizes manifested as a defence mechanism. Denial, repression, regression, displacement, projection. I've felt all these mechanisms in play since being here with a clarity I've never experienced before.'

Rosemary glanced away from the door and across the garden. She listened to a blackbird calling out high up in the conifer and sparrows chattering in the privet hedges.

'What happened to you, lad?'

The scene melted away.

-21-

Scott stirred. His eyes fluttered for a few seconds adjusting to light. A myriad of tiny white flakes floated through the air and a single red leaf fell before him, coming to rest on the grassy slope.

He shook his head and noticed Rosemary standing, head bent a few feet away. She appeared to be examining one of the scarlet leaves.

Without turning, Rosemary raised her head.

'Except for this breeze... well... let's just say... it's the silence. You never quite get used to all the peace. We forget how noisy our world has become.'

Scott eased himself up and walked over, finally surveying the sight before him.

His heart skipped.

All the saliva in his mouth dried up, his muscles were suddenly weak, and his jaw slackened. He blinked then squinted growing dizzy. He stumbled a couple of steps and turned his back on the immense scarlet forest, only to be faced with the eight colossal monoliths.

He shuddered.

'What in the hell? I don't want to know where we are, not just yet, but this is not what I expected,' he muttered.

'Strangely peaceful, and the air... so clean, so fresh. I think I could retire here,' Rosemary glanced at him with a grin. 'Other dimensions can be spectacular. We're not in Kansas anymore.'

She indicated to a monolith not far from where Scott had laid.

'That's our rift door,' she continued. 'That big bugger of ancient stone in front of you. If you look at it, it's a little different from the rest, a little darker wouldn't you say?'

'Yeah. Yeah, I can see. Wait... are those empty boxes?'

'They are indeed. They must have come through from the club at some point.'

'Or thrown through.'

'Perhaps.'

Scott shook his head, 'Have I been asleep? How long was I out for?'

'For a while – and by the way, you were right, it is autumn here. I would surmise that *time* moves a little differently here, a little bit faster.'

'Wait, did you say, time here moves faster?'

'Yes. Changes in our reality will equal a change in time.'

'So...'

'So, it's like one hour here is only one minute back home, that sort of thing.'

Scott rubbed his palms over his face. 'None of this is happening, seriously. Please, tell me I drank too much, that I'll wake up in a second and we can go for fish and chips.'

Rosemary glanced at him. 'Not a chance, sunshine.'

'You're enjoying this aren't you?'

'No, not really but you've got to make the most of things.'

'So, tell me Rosemary, who exactly are you? How do you know so much about... about all this?'

She turned her head away.

'In a bit, eh, Scott? I'm hoping the women somehow came through by accident. That they stumbled in here. We find them and we bring them back. Now, I need you to show me the person you sensed. The one you felt this morning, who you saw before you passed out back in the restroom. The one from your nightmares. I need to know who and what we're dealing with or if it's just another traveller caught up here,' She paused and then she whispered. 'Or maybe I shouldn't do that at all,' she whispered to herself.

'And what in god's name is that?' Scott ignored her and turned to face the second stone structure. Three standing stones with a mammoth top stone.

Rosemary grinned.

'I can tell you what it looks like. It's a dolmen.'

Scott started towards it.

'A what? It looks like a pile of rocks to me.'

'The three stones are megaliths. It's topped off with a capstone. We have them all over our world.'

For a long time, Scott just stood, head up lost in thought.

Rosemary watched him and noticed something she had not seen in the young man before, confidence. She had seen the immense changes that accepting paranormal abilities brought. They could completely change an individual and their personality. Being open to a new reality and a new way of being. It was difficult to keep hold of the old sense of self when you began to see the world with fresh awareness.

She narrowed her eyes. Scott's speed of assimilating psychic skills was both baffling and amazing. Was now the time to confide in him? In someone? To expose her life history as a paranormal?

That someone should be her daughter, Carol. That was if her daughter hadn't already guessed what her mother and father had been up to over the years. Why had she not told her daughter about everything after Henry's death? It was a question that played over in her head repeatedly.

Rosemary sighed.

Scott slowly turned his head.

'The gateway, er... you know the rift. I think I know how it works.'

'You're a plumber or are you a locksmith now?' Rosemary headed over to the darker monolith and circled it, Scott followed.

'No seriously, Rosemary, you told me to listen as I walked into the cubicle, right? I zoned in or whatever you call it. Well, that's what I did and what I got back was a voice telling me it's all to do with vibrations... watch.'

Rosemary raised her hand almost wanting to stop him. 'Careful, take it slow, you're new to this,' she said.

'Careful?' he huffed. 'I think the time for being careful has gone, don't you?'

After a few moments, white light began to shine from the monolith bathing the area around them.

Scott concentrated, his voice once again reverberated as he spoke.

'It's created with... something that sounds like spatial harmonics. The correct adjustment to the frequency opens the rift.'

Rosemary whispered at his shoulder. 'Then we can get back, you can open it? Close it?'

'No, there is a second element, another part to the key to open the rift.'

'Focus gently, Scott, this may take a lot of time, simply listen, reach out for the answer.'

Scott nodded and kept his eyes fixed on the boulder. 'It's an emotion... not sure... harmonics and emotion.'

'And you can open it? Get us home, we don't have to find the mechanism that opens it from here?' Rosemary asked again.

'Yes, I think I can, I don't understand how it all works. Too much information all at once. I need time to listen, to understand it, but I'll try if it will save the women.'

Rosemary turned away with a raised eyebrow. 'We at least have a backup plan for getting home. We could try it now. Leave this instant if you want. Forget the women. Go back through and close the rift from our side?' she waited.

Scott came into view tilting his head to the side attempting to catch a glimpse of her face. She saw him grin.

'That's a waste of time. Something else is here. It also knows how to open the rift so let's just find the women.'

Rosemary turned to Scott with a smile. 'Smart boy,' she replied and pointed toward the nearest triangular buildings. 'Those Japanese-style shrines, let's see what's there.'

She watched him set off.

Her smile disappeared. Her brows drew together. He had managed to adapt and manipulate a rift easily.

Her throat tightened.

She followed.

-22-

Down a small slope and under the canopy of the trees they headed. At the bottom, the strange white mist wrapped around their legs like liquid.

It was cool.

The idea of leaving now was unthinkable. But Rosemary had needed to know Scott's intentions, the person he was, and whether it matched up with what she had encountered in his unconscious mind. His childhood seemed happy and normal but in his later life, the drinking and drugs. What could have driven him to that? Was a past event responsible for that large, impenetrable door deep in his unconscious? Regardless of his past transgressions, his response to locating the women filled her with some hope.

'It makes sense that the women would have headed for shelter and those temple shrine things seem to be the only structures around,' said Rosemary.

'Maybe. It must have been scary just walking through the cubicle and finding they couldn't get back,' replied Scott.

'The door opens both ways. Let's hope they had the sense to head for shelter.'

'What is this mist stuff anyway? Didn't expect it to be so cold. It's everywhere. Is it even safe?'

'I think so. I've seen something similar a couple of times.' She gestured to Scott and took one of his arms as they trod tentatively forward.

'Are we alright here? What I mean is – won't we get contaminated – pick-up bacteria?' Scott asked.

'You mean will we get sick from being in a new dimension without some sort of protective spacesuit?'

'Yeah, I guess that is what I'm asking.'

'You're smarter than you look. Many people wouldn't even consider that. It's unlikely. We're not on another planet. It's another plane and there are doors. Doors to other universes have been open since before man even showed up. There aren't many viruses and germs left that haven't migrated to our world. In fact, some believe a great many of our pandemics have originated from elsewhere. We've adapted to most of them throughout our evolution without even knowing about it,' she explained.

'Something tells me you've been doing this kind of thing for a while. I'm betting you can fill a few nights with stories down at the pub when this is all over.'

'That I could, but I'm more a sit-in-the-house-with-a-cup-of-tea-storyteller. Saying that... I wouldn't turn down a drink and a packet of cheese and onion at my local.'

She watched Scott move his hands around.

'This mist, it's so cold, but the air around us is warm. It's like putting my hands into one of those chest freezers at the supermarket.'

'It's almost like it's part of some atmosphere processing system... like an air conditioner. My Henry worked in that area but the question is... an atmosphere for what and why?'

'Can't you, I don't know, sense the women? I mean, are they even still here? Maybe there was another doorway.'

'I could yes, but I choose not to.'

'What? Why?'

Rosemary threw him a look, 'Trust me.'

They navigated through scarlet trees towards the strange shrine. It was hard going, putting one foot before the other, unable to see the ground beneath. As they walked Rosemary raised the question again.

'Scott, can you describe him to me, the one from your dreams? I know it's hard, luv, but can you give me a visual description?'

'I don't know how,' Scott relied. 'It seems stupid, like telling someone about your dream. I know it isn't a dream now. I'm just a new guy who knows jack shit about the world, it seems.'

Rosemary smiled. 'That's not the way it's always going to be, alright?'

'Someone said something similar to me recently,' Scott smiled back and sighed deeply. 'Right, okay, let me see.

What is... he... like. It must have been about... late February when I had my first dream, and it was the one thing I remembered clearly. He stands over seven feet tall with a cardboard box covering his head. A skinny, creepy long body that's... well... his body is shiny like it's wet. It reminds me of how lobsters and crabs are constructed or the way insects are. He has long fingers almost claws–'

'A box on his head?' Rosemary asked, coming to an abrupt halt, and staring up at him wide-eyed. 'What type of box?'

'A box, a regular plain brown, just like the ones around by the monolith back up there. You know the type they use for dry stock that gets delivered. The lid flaps are spread out over its shoulders,' Scott explained.

'What else? Did you say he? Does he speak?'

'He doesn't say anything, just a low hiss and the sound of the cardboard scraping as it moves against walls. I just feel it's a 'he.' Most of the time it stands there, watching me like some freak but I don't think he knows I'm seeing him. Then I usually wake up. When I saw him in the restroom, it was like... as if for the first time he was staring right back at me, face-to-face, if that makes sense.'

'Face to box.'

'Funny.'

'Face to face,' Rosemary echoed. Her eyes narrowed. 'You've never seen him when you've been awake before?'

'No, and never that close,' Scott stated. 'If I had to put a word to the way he looked at me, even with a box, it would be... curiosity. Yeah, that's it, curiosity. Maybe he's stuck here too?'

Rosemary, now out of breath, paused beneath a tree. She let go of Scott and gazed up into its branches.

'Hmmm, I think I'm beginning to see a pattern here. Things are fitting into place, I think–' She raised her finger.

Before she could say anymore, a shadow fell across her. She spun around and gasped.

A small, dark, thin figure appeared. It rose out of the mists behind Scott like a shark's fin from water.

'Scott!'

Withered hands closed over Scott's face. He struggled but only for a second. His eye closed and he was dragged down beneath the surface.

'Nooo!' Rosemary screamed.

It was too late.

He had gone. Vanished beneath the noiseless, ethereal white of the mist.

-23-

Dan dragged the girl's body into the ladies' restroom and down to the cubicle at the end. He lowered her body to the floor. The girl's head slowly slumped over onto the toilet seat.

He staggered back, breathing heavily and drew his sleeve across his forehead. He held onto the sink and took a few moments to catch his breath before removing his backpack.

The weight of an unconscious body was something that had surprised him. Although he had done it several times, it still amazed him how difficult it was.

Dan unzipped his backpack pulling out a Glock 9mm handgun, which he relocated to his jacket and a plastic food box containing a small bottle, and a wrapped needle and syringe. He tore open the plastic wrapping and filled the syringe. Shaking it, he watched the liquid bounce around in its temporary prison. He held the syringe between his teeth and got down beside the girl.

'Nothing personal, darling, but I got to look out for number one and do the right thing,' he whispered.

He knew once it was done that it would not take long. He just had to close the cubicle door, stand back and wait.

Dan tried not to think about what happened to the young women once they disappeared. The nightmare visions that populated his dreams had prevented any decent sleep for months.

But it was worth it.

It would not take long.

Like clockwork, the cubicle knew to create the strange eerie light.

Over the months, he had noticed the blue light growing stronger. Stretching out like fingers up to the ceiling and out to parts of the next cubicle.

What he was doing was a good thing, he was convinced of that. Not long now and then he was free. Free to put all this behind him.

That bag and that stupid-looking radio. Must be Rosemary's. He shivered, closed his eyes and nodded. They had gone through then. Good, two fewer people to ruin things.

With a dragged-out sigh and ignoring his accelerated breathing, he took the girl's left arm and pulled her jacket sleeve up. Now to find a vein.

I'm going to get away with all this.

-24-

Rosemary desperately swept away at the mist.

'Scott! Scott where... hold on. No, no!'

There was no way Scott could have been carried off without her noticing. Scott would not be easy to haul around.

'Oh god!'

The mist didn't disperse, instead, it rose serpent-like up her arm.

'Get off me!'

She gasped, waving the mist away but each time she did it returned. It wove its way around her body and up to her head teasing her winter white hair. With trembling hands, she breathed out and centred herself. She closed her eyes. Paranormal senses reached out to touch the mist.

She edged backwards.

'What is this, what are you trying to show me? All I'm feeling is a sense of myself, a reflection.'

The mist reacted rapidly spinning and convulsing.

'Reveal more to me.'

The mist rolled and undulated propelling itself a metre away like a squid instinctively reacting to an enemy. It remained part of the moving mass covering the forest floor but now began to form two singular shapes. On the right, a huge human hand manifested its index finger extended.

'Reveal more to me.'

Astonished she watched as a second yet smaller hand formed on the left. Its index finger also extended about to respond to the imminent touch of the other.

The Creation of Adam, she knew it instantly. God stretched out his finger to bestow Adam with life. Michelangelo, Book of Genesis, masterpiece, the *Creation of Adam fresco* on the Sistine Chapel ceiling.

'Why are you showing me this?'

As if responding to her question the hands pulsed, blending like two streams joining a river. The mist rose higher and gradually curled, twisted and contorted till it assumed a shape, a human shape.

Rosemary edged back further.

From behind the central form grew two huge powerful wings.

Her blood ran cold.

'You're showing me my ideology? Reflecting my beliefs about paranormals? Tormenting me? Do you intend to remind me of the ridicule I faced at Green Street? How dare you!' Rosemary shouted at the mass.

The shape collapsed down, re-joining the mist washing over the forest floor.

Everything became peaceful and calm again.

She felt her hands trembling on her chest. Her heart beating fast.

Had that all been real? She was sure it was.

'I have to find Scott,' she whispered.

She trod carefully to the side determined to resume the search. Her foot made a familiar noise on a surface. Metal, a metal surface. A grate of some sort below her. Heart still racing she located the edges beneath the mist. The smooth hard surface was colder than the mist.

Damn!

It was too heavy.

She stood cupping her hands and blew on her fingers.

None of this was even remotely sane..

A forest with beautiful maples, with leaves of scarlet. Wooden Japanese temple-looking buildings peppered like sentinels throughout the forest. Tiny crystal-like flakes endlessly drifting and meandering in the air and the cool mist lying all around. It was like a fairy tale gone wrong.

Silence lay steadily upon it all. A silence that suggested whatever lived here, lived alone.

Wait a minute... the same flurry of white flakes spun in a similar pattern moments ago. A breeze kept coming through the trees. The position of the trees produced a sort of current through which the air flows.

Did she imagine that same pattern? Something was messing with her mind.

She gave it no more thought,

Rosemary had never been one for fanciful events or places. But in her life, she had seen many unusual things. She had hoped that one day it would all make sense. That she would understand the true meaning of all she had witnessed. She had always tried to be scientific as a paranormal investigator. It had given her an air of respectability.

In the realm of the paranormal and supernatural, adherence to scientific laws was not always a given. It had inflicted on her a great deal of heartache and pain. Now as an older woman, those emotions had subsided, yielding to a sense of openness and heightened awareness. Answers weren't always her primary pursuit. The allure now lay in the experience itself. Doubts no longer plagued her. Once wonder in life is discovered, letting go proves to be a challenge.

She turned and steadily made her way towards the shrine. It was the only logical place the women would have headed and maybe there she could get some help to find Scott.

***

Scott opened his eyes. Darkness. Where was this? When was this?

'Shit!' How many more times could he wake up disorientated. The grass bank, the hospital, his parent's house, his apartment, the monolith ring and now this.

He began by trying to stand. He was surrounded by darkness. It was cold and silent. The place reeked of dust and mildew.

His feet scraped on wood, and he dropped to his knees. Crawling forward, he explored with his hands. He struck a wooden board and slid along it until he hit the corner. He tried to breathe steadily, hoping at the same time his eyes would adjust to the darkness.

With a jolt, the room vibrated. Creaking sounds like an old tree makes in a storm echoing through space, bouncing off walls.

Scott felt sick and his stomach gurgled. He smiled to himself, he couldn't believe he was in this situation and his only thought was about how long it had been since he had eaten.

He had changed since he had entered the cubicle. Was entering even his decision? And the voices when he listened. They told him exactly what he needed to know like being plugged into some audio learning network.

He smiled again in the dark with the thought that he was possibly going mad, schizophrenic maybe. The thoughts came flooding. He had an understanding, a rudimentary knowledge of schizophrenia. At some point in his past, he had learned about mental illness. Yet another piece to add to the puzzle.

'I can handle this, I can handle this.'

He had started reciting the mantra on the day he regained consciousness in February. He had forgotten a lot of who he had been before and was still none the wiser about the key figures in his life. He was like a malfunctioning computer. Half of his hard drive was completely wiped. Despite this, he knew without hesitation that none of that mattered, not right now. He had to find Rosemary. For a split second, he knew he was not alone. Then as quickly as the feeling had come, it faded.

'I can handle this.'

Wait!

The figure that had dragged him beneath the mist. His heart began to race.

A hand over his face and mouth. The sick feeling, then finally losing consciousness. Should he listen? Use his newly gained abilities? Could he do it without Rosemary at his side?

A realisation came to him. He may not know who he was, where he was going or how he had ended up in some weird mystical forest, but he knew that Rosemary needed him. She needed him to help stop the cubicle from its expansion and unleashing something dangerous into the world. The women had somehow found their way here or had been brought here and they too may need help.

The continued silence bothered him.

How long had he been out? It was impossible to know. Every second felt like a lifetime.

Scott thought, then made a decision. The feelings he had been exposed to upon entering the cubicle, that wave of strength and curiosity.

Instantly, the fear burned away like water drops on a hot stove, replaced by confidence and assuredness.

He must be in one of the shrines, there'd been nothing else in this godforsaken place. There had to be a door here somewhere.

Scott got to his feet and continued to feel his way along the wall searching for a way out. He found only more wooded panels.

A loud creek echoed through, causing him to inhale sharply, his gaze fixed on the abyssal darkness.

A straight line of light appeared downward cutting through the darkness. Scott watched as the light expanded to reveal a large wooden door being pulled open. Light stabbed at his eyes. He looked away and covered his face with both hands.

A young woman's voice giggled and sang a rhyme.

'I leave a trail because you're blind, I place the leaves for you to find.'

Scott trembled as the hairs on his neck prickled. The least anticipated surprise was encountering a woman who sang a haunting nursery rhyme, her voice a blend of wheezes, giggles and euphoric delight.

Still, his eyes had not adjusted fully, but now he could see the shifting shape of a figure, it stood in front of him.

Then like a light switch being flicked, his vision sharpened and came into focus.

He saw her.

She was a young girl, no more than nineteen. He almost relaxed at the sight of her. It was the woman he had seen in the hallway at the nightclub with Dan.

But something inside him wanted to scream, run and hide at that moment. She was like a wild child. He remembered the term 'wild child' from some past event, school or college. Developmental psychology was it? A person raised in the wild. A feral child. That's what he saw except this woman had been normal once. Her clothes were a patchwork of faded fabrics, once vibrant but now weathered by time and wear. Her blouse, once a delicate pastel hue, was now frayed at the edges, revealing the threadbare nature of the material. Her hair, a dark mess of knots and tangles, cascaded in disarray around her gaunt face. Her posture was wrong, she sniggered and stared at him as if he were a new puppy for her delight.

Within the wooden shrine, Scott stood cocooned by the elegant contour of the architecture. The gables, with their gentle slopes and adorned with intricate markings, soared overhead bestowing a sense of sanctuary. Yet, the wood bore the weight of age, its dark stain casting an atmosphere not of reverence and tranquillity, but rather one of foreboding and neglect.

The room was nonetheless empty.

Past the woman, he glimpsed a balcony its edges uneven and contorted. Beyond stretched the forest with its scarlet maple trees, far below. Surely there were stairs leading down. The shrines had appeared held up by giant supports. No one could leap from this height without injury.

He returned his focus to the girl standing at the door.

'Who are you?' Scott asked, his voice echoing around the room. It didn't sound right.

'The master said I am to... play with you,' a scratchy voice replied. Her eyes flared with excitement. 'Gonna do what he says.'

'Are you one of the women, who went missing from the club? How long have you been here? We're here to help you?'

'Women?'

'Yes, four women from the nightclub. Are you one of the ones who went into the cubicle at the end? Is someone holding you here?'

'Too many questions, questions, questions, but don't fret. You don't need to worry about any of it anymore.'

An unsettling blend of joy and malevolence etched across her skeletal face surged a wave of panic within him. He took a deep breath and forced himself to accept that he was the adult in this situation. The woman was unstable, brainwashed or worse.

'Seriously,' he said stepping forward. 'You're gonna play the cryptic response routine with me, darlin? Looking like you just heaved yourself up out of a flamin sewer?'

The woman's eyes widened. She stepped forward into the room. 'You ain't scared anymore, I prefer them when they're scared, and so does my master. I can see into their heads, see their fears and make them grow,' she circled him like a predator. 'Please... please become afraid again...for me.'

'Not going to happen. Where's Rosemary? Where's the person I came here with? What have you done with her?'

The young woman just pointed at him and began to laugh.

'How can you laugh? I asked you a question. Where is my friend, where is she?'

His face dropped. Nothing would come of questioning this wild woman. It was useless. He had to find Rosemary and get away. Without another word, he made for the open door, but the woman shrieked and leapt upon him.

-25-

Amidst the haunting fog of the forest, consumed by the fear of never seeing her family again, Rosemary stood, closed her eyes, and embraced the gentle breeze upon her skin. Purposefully summoning memories, she recalled encounters that had evoked similar emotions within her.

It was while studying the maple forest now with a gentle warm breeze touching her skin that Rosemary recalled a memory. A trip to the New Forest National Park in Hampshire. Carol was only a child and Henry's love for the great outdoors had brought endless camping holidays into their lives. It was funny how in times of fear and uncertainty she brought forward memories to act as a balm. How comforting, that she should be reminded of that time now. An easier, happier time to recall when faced with the possibility of never seeing her family again.

She had faced death more than once in her career. Drawing strength from memories was a powerful method to forge a path forward when faced with difficult obstacles.

Her thoughts went to Scott.

Who took him?

Who was that withered figure?

Were they also trapped here unable to get out?

Rosemary paused, head tilted, hand waving as she traced threads of thought. She had simply stepped through the rift to this forest dimension without any thought of risk. Moreover, she had taken an innocent civilian whom she barely knew. Surely this was suicide, so why had she behaved in this manner? The questions flicked across her face like shadows on a wall. Her eyes widened and the spark of answers crystalised in her mind. Green Street. Was she so upset at being asked to leave by the ghost-hunting group that she would act so recklessly? Or was she trying to make a statement that at sixty-seven she was still useful?

She clenched her jaw and breathed slowly. There was little point in worrying. She had a job to do, the job always came first. Find the women, stop the bad guy and locate Scott on the way because, without him, she wasn't entirely sure her abilities could help her leave this place.

***

The woman's piercing scream echoed as she thrust her elbow into Scott's face, sending him stumbling backwards. A forceful sidekick struck his chest, leaving him sprawled on the floor, astonished by the fierce strength and agility of the young woman.

With a shriek, she targeted him again, launching herself into the air. Scott's instincts kicked in and he rolled to the right, narrowly avoiding her landing. She snarled and snapped at him like an animal, prompting him to rise and bolt for the safety of the open door.

The woman pursued him relentlessly, moving with an almost primal agility across the floor. With a burst of energy, she hurled herself through the air, wrapping her pale arms around his legs and bringing him down.

He fought back, kicking out as she clawed and thrashed, attempting to reach his vulnerable neck and face. He managed to seize her wrists and leveraging his strength, rolled her over, pinning her beneath him. Scott, though a fit, young man recognised that her outward appearance of fragility could have easily misled him into underestimating her. As they locked eyes, he noticed a predatory glint, her lips curving into an anticipatory smile.

Expecting a bite or being spat at, he braced himself. Then, in a sudden shift, her muscles relaxed and she simply stared, her wide eyes exuding a menacing intensity. Scott's eyes blinked rapidly, unsettled by her unnaturally motionless state. A jolt ran through him. He sensed a presence, malevolent tendrils of her consciousness creeping in. She was there, probing and seizing control of his mind.

***

Rosemary stepped into the clearing, her eyes fixated on the imposing structure before her. Her intuition had been correct. The building stood on colossal wooden pillars firmly rooted into the earth. Intrigued, she meticulously scrutinised every detail, studying each feature with precision, looking for information she could use to understand this peculiar and unfamiliar place. The wooden building reminded her of Japanese shrines, the timber-framed exterior being strikingly similar. It stood about 11 by 6 metres and included a raised floor, verandas around the building and a staircase leading to a single central doorway straddled by intricately carved pillars. The tall triangular design of the roof was particularly impressive with gentle curves supported by smaller posts and lintels.

She stepped closer. The intricacy of the wood, the designs and how it had been prepared – impressive indeed. Every inch of the wood's surface had been engraved with symbols from an unknown language. The place was old, very old.

A warm breeze blew into the clearing. She inhaled, needing to get back to the task at hand, she thought.

'Scott?' Rosemary called.

No answer, nothing.

A flight of steps rose to a veranda. She felt a presence. Was it one of the women, Amy, Gemma, Nadine or Abbi? Four steps up she held her breath.

She stopped and listened.

Why had she not realised it before?

No sound. No sound from the forest. A repetitive gush of wind through the trees now and then. Where are the birds? The insects? There had to be some animal life! Surely. Nothing. How had she not noticed that?

As if to reward her for the realisation, her head moved towards a new sound.

She listened.

Was it murmuring? Yes, slow and steady. It seemed to reach a hiss.

Then silence.

She remained on the fourth step.

'Hello?' she called. 'Is there anyone here?'

Rosemary could use her psychic abilities to locate Scott and the women. It was tempting. Just close her eyes, focus and listen... but no – not yet. She was too afraid of what she might find.

She walked up the remaining stairs. Each step groaned and creaked under her weight.

Reaching the veranda, she walked toward a sombre entrance framed by two engraved timber pillars, standing tall and formidable like guardians, evoking an aura reminiscent of sentries to the underworld. Her lips formed silent words tracing echoes of previous thoughts. She had been right, there was no actual door here just an opening, and there was no straight lintel. The way in was rectangular with a rounded top, like a church window.

She passed through.

Rosemary's shoulders tensed, her hands instinctively flying to cover her mouth. Her expectations of a serene sanctuary were swiftly shattered by the reality before her. Rather than the anticipated tranquillity, the autumn light pierced through ceiling cracks, casting an eerie amber glow across an expansive, desolate space. Sharp sword-like patterns painted the floor as light streamed through fractured panels in the walls, creating an unsettling atmosphere. A far cry from the peaceful refuge she had envisioned.

Wincing, she tightened her hand across her mouth and nose. A pungent sharp smell made her feel sick. It mirrored the nauseating stench of a butcher's market, only amplified to an intolerable degree, causing her stomach to churn. With each step, the aged floor creaked beneath her weight, and she felt her shoes stick to the grimy, blackened surface, each movement a disconcerting reminder of the space's neglected state.

She couldn't see far into the room, and her eyes were slow to adjust.

Eventually, something caught her eye to the right.

Clothes... clothes lay on the floor, but not scattered... placed. A blue shiny top. Jeans with a silver belt, pink lacy underpants, and cream slip-on shoes. Rosemary bent down. She knew she could touch them, reach out and find something out about these clothes, but she chose not to. More clothes there on her left. These are the women's clothes. They have to be but where are they?

Something moved, stirring in the darkness at the edge of her vision. She froze almost wishing she hadn't seen it.

One, two, three, she counted in her head. Then straightened up and trod further into the room. Shadows shifted around her, every step an endless groan beneath her weight. More clothes were tidily laid out on either side of her now. Bunches of keys, phones, hairbrush, handbags and an e-cigarette.

She wanted to leave. To turn and run, head back through the rift, go home, lock the door. Surround herself with the comforts of home.

Determination surged within her, overriding the urge to flee. She couldn't abandon her role as an investigator, the thought alone was unbearable. Finding the four missing young women was the mission. Her commitment to getting them back to their families outweighed any personal risk. Even if it meant confronting the worst, she vowed to see it through, willing to sacrifice everything, even her own life to ensure their safe return,

She approached the back end of the room. The atmosphere became thick and warm. This end part was darker still. She looked towards the shadowy end wall.

A dark figure detached itself from the gloom.

A shadowed, sinewy man shape. A box covered its head. It was turned away from her like a punished child. Maybe it hadn't noticed her? She knew that was not possible.

It had always known she was there.

Rosemary squinted. Old eyes attempted to focus on the shape; its body... looked moist.

Were those clothes it wore? Wet clothes – or was that its body, its skin?

The box stirred, revealing slender wisps of feathery hair slipping out from underneath as it pivoted, gradually aligning to meet her gaze.

They stood in silence.

-26-

The world swirled and refocused.

Scott stood at the main entrance to a hospital. He tried to appear purposeful and read the various signboards. Accident and Emergency, Maternity, Radiography.

At his side was the young woman in her late teens, blonde and petite.

'None of them seems to fit what we're looking for,' Scott said, reading.

'Maybe it's one of those special places, what do they call them?'

'ICU,' he replied. 'Intensive Care.'

'Let's look there then.'

'They won't allow visitors into ICU unless they're a close family member,' Scott stated. 'I'm sure I heard that.'

'Nonsense,' the woman snapped. 'I don't believe they'd refuse you.'

They sauntered into the hospital's main corridor. It was just an ordinary hospital except there were no people. He passed the main reception area, with the woman trailing behind, heading toward a coffee shop, that to his dismay, also sat empty.

Where was everybody?

Down a wide corridor, they peered curiously through small windows set in wide double doors that led to other wards and treatment rooms.

Scott stopped in his tracks. A brown-grey rabbit hopped about the corridor floor. It seemed unaware of them for a moment then it turned and looked up at him with shining obsidian eyes.

'Why is there a rabbit here?' the woman asked.

'I have no idea,' Scott replied.

The rabbit continued to glare at Scott with its large eyes. With one flick, it jumped, turned and flashed its white tail. It vanished around a corner.

'Should we go after it?' the woman asked.

'No! It's the wrong time,' Scott whispered instinctively, not sure why he said it.

They continued. Walking around the hospital was making Scott weary, especially when coupled with the woman's constant questions. He began to wonder, not for the first time, what he was doing here.

He felt lost and alone. Alone... empty... as empty as the corridors in a hospital that were both familiar and unknown to him. Nothing new, he thought.

Something crept into his mind, unrecognisable yet known.

He was drawn down another sterile, white corridor following the signs for the stairs. Ignoring the woman, he made his way through the door.

The stairway led up or down.

He knew the woman sensed his uncertainty. She stepped in front of him.

'Is this the way? Is this the way we need to go... to find it?'

'I don't know. I... I can't see.' He started down the stairway the woman followed.

He didn't know how long they walked down – minutes, hours? The stairs finally terminated in an empty, dimly lit corridor.

They continued through swinging doors that squealed open into other deserted corridors. Finally, at the very end of one was a single wooden door. It pulsed with light as they approached it.

He heard the woman breathe nervously behind him as he reached out for the handle. The door swung open silently before he had a chance to touch the handle.

He glanced at the wide-eyed woman.

'I think this is it... but who are we here to see... I've forgotten?'

'Someone, someone you know, someone who has been kept from us,' the woman whispered.

Even deeper shadows engulfed the room, where the potent scent of dust and wood permeated the air. His struggling eyes saw a room filled with boxes. Some cardboard, some wooden, some colourful and childish, all piled in symmetrical order. Shelves full of packages both modern and dusty with age. Is that a Red *Power Ranger* helmet? A white and black *Furby* toy? And that, a small blue egg-shaped device attached to a key ring. He reached out and took the *Tamagotchi*. Moving it around in his hand he glanced up at a faded poster for the film *Wayne's World*.

Stepping carefully further into the room he lifted the lid on a box. *He-man and the Masters of the Universe* action figures. There was no reason for this place, no explanation. These toys and objects were ones of value to someone.

No!

How can this be right?

He raced down the room opening box after box, all full of books and toys. This can't be.

Stopping, he stepped back. He recognised who these objects belonged to.

I have to be sure, he thought.

Scott moved deeper into the room.

He sorted through VHS cassettes each labelled in different handwriting, *The Fresh Prince of Bel-Air* – *Saved by the Bell* – *Toy Story 2* – *The Incredibles* – *Blockbusters*. He smiled as he held CDs of Usher and Jamiroquai. With all the exploring, he had forgotten the woman was in the room until she broke the silence.

'Is this–'

'Yes,' Scott interrupted, 'this... all of this... is me.'

-27-

Rosemary retrieved a piece of paper from her pocket with trembling hands, unfolding it, struggling to read the words in the dim light, yet realising she already knew the names written on the paper.

'Amy Mansell, Abbi Price.' She was ashamed of herself for the way her voice shook. 'Nadine Bladon, Gemma Moles.' She tucked the paper, back into her pocket. 'Where are they?'

No answer.

She knew she was shaking and swallowed hard. Her pulse raced. 'Wait! You're in my head, in my mind,' she said.

'Wait! You're in my head, in my mind,' echoed the box-headed figure, the voice deep and velvety emanating from within the confines of the cardboard box.

'Where are they?' Rosemary asked.

There were no features for her to read. Box-Head's heavy breathing was the only indication it was alive.

'Where are they?' Rosemary repeated. 'The women?'

Elongated hands slowly moved. Long gnarled fingers unfolded in snaps and clicks. Hands came to rest on its dark chest. *'The women,'* it repeated, *'are part of me now.'*

Rosemary staggered and a sob escaped her lips.

Box-Head remained motionless as if studying her.

'You've killed them!' She gasped, holding the base of her throat. 'Four innocent young lives.'

Box-Head titled its head in curiosity. *'You care?'*

'You're in my head! Of course, I care. They were people. Why? Why did you kill them?'

'Because I could,' it replied.

Rosemary balled her fists and held her breath for several seconds. She exhaled, surprised at the tension leaving her body. She gazed once more at the clothes on the floor. If she was being honest with herself she had known the answer already. But to hear it...

She closed her eyes.

'...and Scott?'

'*The male, he is nearby... with one of mine. However, I am much more interested in you... Rosemary.*'

The way it said her name, stretching it out with its deep calm voice chilled her.

'*Fascinating. Here you stand in front of me, a creature, a being you have never seen before, outside of your world and your only thoughts are to ask about others.*'

It moved slowly holding the back wall to steady itself, its breathing heavy and laboured.

'Why?' Rosemary muttered. 'Why take them? What exactly do you want with the women?'

'*I have brought females through the breach. They are young; they are seeping, swollen with regret and self-loathing and at such a young age. It is inconceivable for me to imagine a species that allows its young to grow this way. I have wanted to meet an older female for such a very... very long time.*'

'Who and what are you?'

'*I am beyond you, old woman, I have...*' the box moved, it suggested realisation, '*Ah! I see you are not like others of your kin. You fear me, yes, I can smell it, but not in the same way. You have seen a great many things. Done a great many things. Let me in further, Rosemary.*'

'No. I'll stop you.'

'*No, you will not.*'

Rosemary cried out. A burning sensation cut through her body. She clasped her hands over her stomach. She felt herself topple over.

'*Your male is separated from you. Where will you go? Everything you have done, the wonders you have seen. You have a lifetime of emotion to give, so no! You will not be leaving and you will nourish me for years.*'

***

Scott gazed longingly around.

'This all belongs to me. My memories, my life, my childhood... well, some of it and other stuff is... well into my teens, but it is me... it's all mine.'

His focus was drawn to a large black trunk resting on the floor concealed in the shadows. There was nothing especially impressive about it. No distinct marks or significant memory attached to it.

He saw that the woman's attention had now been captivated by it. She pushed him out of the way to better see the container. She lowered herself down and drew her hands across it softly caressing the edges. She closed her eyes and sighed, long and hard.

'There's a name here inscribed on the front,' she said.

'What does it say?'

Phae... Phaedrus Cast...er Phaedrus Castellanos.'

Scott edged away from the trunk. The girl slowly moved her head up to face him. She opened her eyes, gleaming with a joyful intensity as she fixed her gaze upon him.

'What have we here?' she said. 'You are strong. Stronger than the others, but you... you've kept me locked out with all those corridors... so many long, empty corridors. But the end is always the same. Time wears down the defences of everyone. It's all just a matter of waiting.'

She continued to caress the trunk.

Scott frowned. Was this woman seriously going psycho? He stepped further away as the woman repeatedly glanced at the trunk and then back at him smiling.

'But this, I didn't expect this, Scott. Such a dark area that you've locked away. Strange how even you don't appear to recognise it anymore and the name, Phaedrus Castellanos. You act as if you have never heard it before and yet it's part of you. This is what I've come here to find and now I have this... I have you.' She returned her attention to the trunk producing a series of small, excited shrieks. Her voice held a chilling calmness, 'What happened to you to create such a beautiful thing as this?' She paused, eyes fixed on Scott. As if inviting him in, she continued, 'Do you want to see what's inside Scott?' With deliberate movements, she withdrew her arms from the trunk, the air seeming to grow heavier. The trunk, an enigmatic vessel, stood before them, its secrets tantalisingly veiled. 'My master has shown me how to rip out, extract and taste fear – to feel it. Fear makes him feel good too,' she murmured, the words dripping with an eerie anticipation.

Finally, she reached for the lid, the hinges groaning in reluctant surrender. The contents lay hidden, poised to reveal the culmination of her revelations.

'No! Please don't.' Scott sobbed. He stepped toward the woman.

She ignored him and started forward, leaning further over into the trunk, only to be brought to a sudden halt. She whirled, glazed eyes easily devoured the contents consuming everything hungrily. She laughed and shrieked.

Scott threw himself at her, but the effort left him drained, causing him to collapse onto the floor.

'Quite the revelation, isn't it? The consequences... your entire life... forgiveness will be difficult and will probably tear you apart. You've been able to open doors to other worlds for such a long time. So much resentment, anger, and hatred,' she remarked quietly, with almost a tinge of sorrow in her voice. 'A wooden signpost atop a cliff. It says Morthoe... What is a Morthoe? What significance does it hold? It's baffling, isn't it? Her posture froze abruptly. 'Ah! This is peculiar... to have your parents disprove of you, yet you seem not to recognise them.'

Kneeling, Scott listened to her words and let out a long-controlled sigh. Tentatively he rose, casting his eyes back to the objects he had grown up with and sensing their strength through memory. These treasures, he remembered and loved. There was a comfort in them, a familiarity... a power. Something he no longer recognised in his present life.

His shoulders fell as he stared with affection at the boxes and packages, finally bringing his gaze back to the woman. He closed his eyes.

'Lies, lies, lies, I've never been able to open doors or rifts or whatever the hell you want to call it. Not till a few days ago. You're just trying to make me angry, lose control or make me think I'm crazy.'

The memory flashed in his mind of the day he awoke on the riverbank... the panic and confusion. The countless times he had woken disorientated with hundreds of voices swimming around in his mind. The loss of a life he had long forgotten and might never remember again, strangers claiming to be family and friends. Neighbours, who gave him a wide berth in the street. Where were the regular memories a person should have? They were absent from that day he had woken on the riverbank.

He remembered the visions of a creature with a box covering his head. He'd dismissed it as his brain trying to make sense of his desperation, his anger. To lose the very thing that makes you human, your identity, your personality, who you are in the world.

Now he had a choice, give up and be swallowed by a storm of animosity and confusion regarding his past or step up, take control, and embrace this new undiscovered country. Rosemary had shown him that he could do extraordinary things. She and Annie both believed in him, they had faith in him, and right now that was enough.

Like a wave crashing up and over a rock, he reached out with his mind.

-28-

Rosemary struggled to her knees as the pain subsided. Then she froze, unable to move but able to speak.

'No! What are you doing?' she asked, her voice cracking.

Box-Head drew closer, moving awkwardly along the floor.

Rosemary strained to lift her hands, but they remained rooted despite her efforts. With every passing moment, the creature edged nearer, inching closer and closer. Inches from her face the cardboard box stopped. All she could hear was its deep wheezing and the rancid smell it carried.

The box slowly moved side to side in a figure of eight. *'They urinated,'* it whispered. *'The girls you spoke of, they were wet with fear. It... excites me.'*

'Do not touch me,' Rosemary said.

'Bold words,' a black finger reached out and caressed her cheek, *'for a woman at the end of her life. A woman barely able to stand, let alone challenge me. That is what you intended to do, was it not?'*

It paused as if hearing a voice.

'I feed off regret, sweet desperation, the missed opportunities of others. They are the fuel that gives me life. Your world is gorged and dripping with it.'

It caressed her hair with the tip of his cracked nail.

'The females brought to me, their bodies polluted with toxins and hate. Each of them despising for how they appear, how they sound, the colour of their skin... their hair. They all wished they had done things differently, all laden with regret and sadness. Your ilk is milk and honey to mine and now, here you stand Rosemary. With you, my strength will increase. I will soon be able to leave this place and feed on your whimpering docile cattle-kind.'

One long disfigured hand waved casually around in the stale air. The other unfurled a crooked blackened finger that scraped down the side of the box in a slow intentional movement.

'Show me your life, Rosemary. The choices you did not make. That house you never brought, the one by the river, do you remember?'

The creature began a gentle intoxicated sway.

'The police career you ruined because... why did you ruin it, Rosemary? Aarrh, the yellow dress you wanted as a child. You hated your mother so much because they could not afford it. The child you never had, an infant son that died.'

It paused, its voice became low and drawn.

'The mist here manifests your dominant unconscious thoughts, those which eat away at you. An unforeseen side effect of my abilities but a welcome one nonetheless. An appetiser you might say of what is to come. What would Henry say... to see you like this? And all those years, Rosemary, all those lost years you could have spent with him. All those stretched-out lonely nights, untouched, unloved.'

'You're sick, twisted...' Rosemary breathed through gritted teeth. Tears welled in her eyes.

'Look to your own kind for a definition of sick and twisted.'

It withdrew and turned.

'I have been watching your world for a long time. With the deteriorating mental state of your kind, I find it difficult to understand why you don't simply demand to be fed upon.'

'Please... don't do this,' Rosemary said.

'What did you expect to find here, old woman?'

'Those girls you fed off, draining them of their future. You could have found another way,' she panted. 'You didn't have to butcher needlessly! Stop this now. We can find another way, an alternative. I'm asking as one person to another.'

'There is little guilt in feeling regret and sadness. When I uncover your shame, it will bring about my continued future. How could you not want that?'

It stood tall, arms open wide.

'This is survival, nothing more. What happens when you starve a creature of its prey? It simply looks elsewhere. Your world is perfect. Pain and missed opportunities cause sweetness of the emotions and subsequently, the meat and I have every right to survive.'

'My world isn't perfect, it's anything but perfect, but we try, we learn and we have achieved so much.'

'Your sin is that your kind is allowed to continue breeding.'

The creature swept down to face her again.

'Your sin, Rosemary, has got you and your kind noticed by others, not of your world. Are you so short-sighted to think that I am the only one?'

Rosemary closed her streaming eyes. She thought of home, Carol and George.

***

Scott listened.

He remained motionless for several more seconds. Finally, he cocked an eyebrow.

'I wonder why I chose this place. A hospital? I'm fed up with bloody hospitals!'

With frightening ease, the young woman looked away from the trunk. She turned, her brow furrowed. For all her casual arrogance, she showed an expression of confusion and sudden realisation.

Scott stared at her.

She seemed calm now, but he could not escape the feeling that one wrong word would trigger her primal anger.

'You're another woman from *Euphoria*, aren't you? A fifth victim of the cubicle. Maybe the first one? One that wasn't reported missing. You were brought to the club in the daytime, you were in such a state. You collapsed in the corridor. I saw you, a vision of you. You were led or taken into that restroom, to the cubicle at the end, through to this forest, to him, to this box-headed man.'

He had to do this quickly. If the heat that rose within him was any indication, he would not be able to think rationally for much longer. He stepped forward.

'But you're not a victim, are you? You're just sick. You were probably chosen because you're... well, nasty, a thief, selfish! Does anyone miss you? Is that why you were chosen.'

The woman stared at him, her eyes glazed over, and her bottom lip trembled.

'Yes,' continued Scott, 'I've recently found that I'm a little bit more than your average plumber. It's about time I showed you just how different, because my new friend, Rosemary, the one you separated me from, seems a real, sweet old lady, and well... I'm getting just a bit fed up with being kicked around like some bloody football.'

The woman swallowed. She stood and wrapped her arms around herself.

Scott stepped forward. His muscles tightened.

'I'm going to ask this just once,' he murmured, a brief thin smile crossing his face before the rage came out. 'Get out of my head!'

The room began to vibrate and what little of the walls could be seen, came apart like plates of ice. Fragments of his belongings sheared off and flew high, and spears of pure light lanced across the room.

The woman screamed and threw herself to the floor.

The room washed away and the scene returned to the dark wooden interior. The same room with a single opening leading to a veranda.

The woman, draped once more in her tattered and frayed garments hissed and snarled with ferocity. She rolled and scrambled away. She rose and looked back at him. But the intensity of Scott's gaze had the young woman screaming.

'You! Who are you?' she shrieked, waving her arms as if he was trying to grab her. 'Why are there two of you? Demons, wraiths, spirits, ghosts and sirens, jinns, artefacts, so many monsters, you know them all, and they know you! Fear you!

His face expressionless, Scott remained standing. He narrowed his focus and kept his eyes locked with hers.

She met his stare as she staggered back through the doorway onto the veranda unable to understand what was happening. Panic and confusion overwhelmed her.

'My master... help – help me!'

His gaze caught her eyes, widening in desperation. Abruptly she halted, holding her breath. In an instant, she directed a pointed finger at him before letting out a piercing scream, toppling backwards and crashing into the wooden veranda rails. The brittle wood splintered and gave way under the sudden force, sending her tumbling down. The sound of the splintering rails echoes, briefly, followed by the thud of her impact below.

As she thrashed about the floor, her movements frantic and unpredictable, the strange mist began to coil and swirl around her trembling form. Her jerking movements slowed, becoming sporadic, before she abruptly went still. The mist enveloped her body, shrouding her in a haze that seemed to swallow her whole. The once tumultuous scene now held an eerie silence.

-29-

The time was right.

Rosemary reached out, surprised to immediately sense Scott in another shrine. The involvement with a strange, wild woman, all flooded through her. She watched as they fought until the woman staggered back and fell to her death.

'Scott,' Rosemary whispered.

Box-Head coughed and began swaying once more.

'A fully-grown human with a lifetime of regret. You will make me strong, Rosemary. Feed me your hatred, your missed opportunities. Let regret hurt you one final time.'

It unfolded decayed fingers and began to wrap them around Rosemary's head.

Box-Head froze. The ragged breath ceased. Its entire body flung backwards, crashing into the rear wall. A roar of agony filled the room.

'Thank you for your concern about my feelings. I will be extremely careful,' Rosemary stated. She pushed her hair back into place with a sigh of relief and struggled to her feet. She dusted herself down before staring at Box-Head.

'It's okay, you can get up now. I have everything I need from you,' she said.

Box-Head remained unmoving in the shadows.

'Oh, the look on your face. Oh, silly me, if only you had a face instead of some elementary cardboard box.' She held her hands behind her back and rocked back and forth.

'Which reminds me, which supermarket did they get it from? Couldn't they have thought of something a little more creative to cover your head?'

Box-Head clawed at the wall attempting to stand but instead stumbled back to the floor.

'You're in my head, do you remember me saying that?' asked Rosemary.

'How did this happen? How can you have... You know nothing!' Box-Head wheezed.

'I reckon I know enough since I've been digging through your brain for the last few minutes. Only seemed fair.' She waved a hand. 'And don't bother with your paralyses trick, it doesn't work very well, not on the likes of me anyway.'

Box-Head raised both hands. It began to claw at the air faster and faster.

Rosemary just stood and watched.

'You cannot feed on me. So how about you stop with the angry kitten impression because, unlike the young women you abducted, terrified and killed without remorse, I do not have regrets.' She said. 'I do not wallow in the missed opportunities of my life. Instead, I have learned to accept them, I've made peace with them. I don't think you researched my kind well enough at all. A woman at the end of her life, a woman barely able to stand, let alone challenge you? That's what you said to me. A woman who made it through from her world to this one. A woman who now stands in front of you, who knows and understands why you prey on the vulnerable and the weak. You cover your face and hide in the background in the dark corners. *She* is laughing at the grandest joke of all time. You're no more than a spoilt child having a tantrum against your peers.'

'*You know nothing... You dare speak of my people... Do you have any idea who I am? Who is before you?*'

'I know that you hate them, you despise them for your incarceration. I'm in your head too, remember? I know they revolted against you. They covered your head as the ultimate disgrace as your customs and rules dictate, despite who you are and what you mean to them.'

Box-Head hissed. It finally stood to its full height. It dwarfed Rosemary and began to sway once again.

'*Are we so different?*' Box-Head leant forward. '*You were abandoned by your group, thrown out, discarded for being old, for being different. We are similar, Rosemary. I too have been abandoned and thrown away. They made me suffer as they did you!*'

The voice beneath the box began to rise.

'We are the same, you and I. Let me spare you as I will spare my kind despite the injustice brought upon me. You fear your age, how useless you have become and whether you will ever be needed again. Join me and all that will forever change.'

Rosemary turned her head back to check the exit.

'We are nothing alike you and I. You've never even met anyone like me, have you? I'm an adult, yes, you're quite correct there and I'm a damn good representative of my species too, if I say so myself. I'm going to ask you one final time. Stop all this now.'

'Or what? You are indeed unique, Rosemary, but you know what I have already done to my people, and what I can do now. My kind must pay for their impudence... you know deep down I cannot and will not cease. Destiny is a silent companion, but mine nonetheless.'

Rosemary's shoulders dropped. She shook her head. 'I didn't think so, but I had to ask, I had to have some hope. I haven't the strength nor the stomach to do what I need to do. But know this,' she jabbed a finger towards Box-Head unsure whether it could even see it, 'many in my world will not hesitate, and by all that's good and right, the relevant people will know. They will know, about you. You've underestimated my kind as so many others have done in the past. And those with the will to fight and defend... they will be waiting.'

Box-Head stopped his sway and leaned back. It started to grunt steadily.

Rosemary cautiously edged backwards.

The Box-Head began to twist as if being attacked in slow motion. Abruptly it let out a loud, deep-toned gurgle grabbing at the rear wall. Its body became rigid as clawed hands gripped tightly shut. It launched into spasms that contorted its body. It became a creature in agony letting out a nerve-chilling scream.

Rosemary staggered, clutching her chest.

Box-Head jerked forward. A thick grey stringy fluid burst from beneath the cardboard box and splattered to the floor. Trailing pieces hung off the edges. After a moment the creature fell to its knees, where it wheezed and struggled. Its heavy breath began to slow. The cardboard box became still for a moment. A rancid stench drifted towards Rosemary as Box-Head rotated slowly towards her.

'What have you done to me?' Box-Head asked.

Rosemary could not answer. It was time to leave and find Scott.

Box-Head made no further attempt to stop her. How could it? Physically it was weak, that much was obvious. She could only imagine how many more lives Box-Head would need to gain its full strength. She had given it a choice.

Now Scott would have to try and close the rift from this side, which meant a limited window of time to cross back home before it closed. She needed to move quickly.

She carefully took small steps away. 'And you're going to need a new box, that one is getting a bit wet.' She kept her eyes on Box-Head until she was sure it wasn't following. With one more glance at the clothes of the young women whose lives had ended here, she left the shrine.

***

On the floor, Scott hesitated.

The room was still full of wood and shadow. He rubbed his temples. *A headache, that's all I need. I have to get out, can't be in here any longer, get out, get out!* The need to flee spun around his head like a spinning top. He rose and cautiously exited through the opening. With shaking hands, he picked his way around the frail veranda till he found steps leading down.

At the bottom, he stood next to one of the huge wooden supports. The cool mist engulfed his lower legs as a suggestion came to him like a voice calling, directing him. He shook his head but found he took steps towards the voice.

'Rosemary,' he whispered.

***

Rosemary cast occasional glances over her shoulder, determined to divert her mind from the potential capabilities of Box-Head and the looming dilemma of the rift back home. If the club's demolition continued, the rift, already exposed, would destabilise and expand.

Right now, Box-Head could barely stand let alone enter a dimensional rift. It needed more strength before it could make the trip through. Even Scott, a robust and healthy young man, succumbed to unconsciousness after passing through. In this dimension she and Scott were possibly the sole inhabitants, making them the solitary source of sustenance.

The moment she had reached out into Box-Head's mind she was also made aware of Scott's plight.

The fifth woman Scott had confronted, what if this Box-Head could feed off the bodies of the dead?

She shuddered.

It would not be the first creature she had encountered that did. With a sense of urgency, she knew they needed to distance themselves from Box-Head, least become prey to an insatiable hunger.

***

Upon reaching the final step down, milky white mist rose from the area where the woman had fallen. It erupted violently, twirling heavenward. No discernible shape just a dance of artistry and swirls.

What was that?

For an instant, in the mist, he glimpsed the shape of a Christmas tree as if sketched by a child. Then the mist gently descended.

He didn't want to think about what the woman had said to him, nor how she had screamed and fallen.

Scott walked away from the shrine. He couldn't look back. Unsure of his direction he walked between scarlet trees, the low mist parting as he went. He squinted and searched the forest through the white myriad of crystal flakes.

He continued forward feeling a strange sensation as if he had passed from being outside into a building.

A sound vibrated in his mind.

The sound became a suggestion.

He pinched the bridge of his nose. It was fear, he decided, like someone watching him.

He spun quickly to glare in one direction. Nothing, only trees.

There it was again.

He walked on for some time, the suggestion in his head urged him forward. In another smaller forest clearing, Scott slowed turning in every direction. A voice seemed to come from all sides.

He paused.

The voice seemed to echo in the surroundings. He scanned the area, finding it eerily vacant. Suddenly, something grabbed his attention and he sprinted towards it.

-30-

Box-Head lumbered slowly, each movement resembling a struggle through thick sand. Yet its actions held a purpose. The mist, hanging low, twisted and curled as it advanced.

In the dim light of the forest, its form gleamed like a finely wrought suit of ebony armour, slender and intricately linked. With little energy left, its needle-like arms dangled at its sides, shoulders slumped, and the box head soaked in bile sagged low.

Familiarity with this forest coursed through its veins, yet the last time it had trod this specific path eluded its memory.

It knew the intruder's destination. It had permitted their entry through the rift, driven by an insatiable curiosity that had nearly exacted a grave toll.

Now, comprehension settled in.

Countless hours were spent widening the minutest chinks in the fabric of reality. Was this destiny? A solitary course laid out solely for it?

One chink became a crack and the crack became a rift, a fissure gaping into another realm, a realm of men.

Then came indescribable elation.

In that newfound world resided minds, malleable and ripe for corruption. Their hunger for greed paralleled their need for air.

Luring a human soul through the rift proved effortless, a siren's call repeated time and again. Someone willing to provide the sustenance it craved. Imagining the faces of its kin upon discovering their captive's vanishing act was a source of profound satisfaction.

Gaining strength in the human realm marked the next phase, propelling it forward until the day it would reclaim what was rightfully its by birth. With the arrival of the two intruders into its forest, everything hung in the balance. The hope of feasting on abundance, a lifetime of festering resentment, teetered on the precipice.

Underestimating them was a mistake it would not repeat.

Beneath the forest canopy, it paused, swaying gently as crystalline fragments descended. Long, dark fingers began to click in a frenzied dance.

A fresh opportunity now beckoned.

-31-

'Rosemary!'

Scott ran towards her. He was never so glad to see a face.

She stood within the mist, calm and reserved. Then her shoulders fell. She opened her arms to receive him. There they stood held together in sobs and relief.

'I killed her, Rosemary. There was another woman, I... she fell and...'

'I know, I know.' Rosemary interrupted. 'I saw it all, I was there with you in your mind as soon as you fought back. I was able to see everything. You didn't kill her, Scott. It wasn't your fault!'

'She got in my head somehow, she – she said things.'

'Let it go, Scott. It was you or her. As soon as you used your abilities, I could reach out, and link with you. I knew you were alright even if I was terrified myself. I couldn't risk psychically calling out to you before, not until I'd confronted Box-Head.'

'Box-Head? You mean the one from my nightmares? You've found him?'

'Yes, and the women are – the girls are dead. He killed them. He fed off them. We were too late.'

'He fed off them?'

She looked away.

They stood in silence.

Like him, the women would have awakened beside the monoliths – terrified, disorientated, and alone. They too, would have been pursued by a creature, knowing they would probably never embrace their families again. He couldn't help but wonder about the sound of their voices, the clothes they wore, and the songs they had grown to love. It weighed heavily on him, knowing the continued anguish their families would endure.

Was Rosemary thinking of her family?

Scott swallowed hard.

'Is this what it's like? Is this what it is to be a paranormal? Creatures, that feed on people?'

'No, you're seeing the worst side of what this life means.'

'There's a fifth woman, you know?' Scott looked up. 'The woman I was with, the one who fell. I think she may have been the first one to come through.'

'Of course, that would make sense. A woman could have come to Euphoria way before I arrived,' Rosemary replied. 'As soon as I linked with you, I saw her through your eyes. I'm so sorry luv, as paranormals we're not supposed to get in each other's heads. I needed to know you were alive and to signal you to me. You'll have to forgive me but I had to. I'm sorry.'

He nodded.

The forest of red maples appeared to envelope Rosemary and Scott in a tranquil hush. Sunlight filtered through scarlet leaves cast a warm, dappled glow. They stood side by side, the weight of what had happened settling in their minds, rendering them silent.

Scott's gaze was distant, lost in a tapestry of red and gold. His thoughts raced, trying to make sense of the extraordinary events that had unfolded. Beside him, Rosemary's expression was a portrait of contemplation. Her eyes normally so lively, were now pools of introspection.

The quiet was broken only by the soft rustle of leaves as a familiar breeze swept through. Time seemed to stretch, allowing them this moment of stillness to process the magnitude of what they had learned. There, in that pocket of the forest Rosemary and Scott found solace in the shared silence.

'Which way?' Scott enquired at last, his voice steady but tinged with uncertainty.

'I'm not sure. Let's head this way, over there towards those thicker-looking trees, I don't want to be standing around in one place like this.'

She strode ahead of him.

'Did you find out her name?' She called back.

'Sorry, no. But she definitely came from Euphoria. I think I saw her, or at least an image of her, back at the club. The assistant manager, Dan, couldn't see her but I did. She was lying in a corridor.

'So, you were seeing an afterimage of her, not a ghost. She was alive here which is why you saw it. Sounds like a residual echo or maybe an unconscious cry for help?'

'I guess if I knew what any of that meant.'

'She was probably the first. But why would Box-Head keep her alive? Companionship? To study?'

Scott glanced over at her and blew out. He pulled his fingers through his hair. 'No idea. He's still here I can feel him now. It... him... this Box-Head, whatever it is.'

'Once I knew you were alright, Scott, I knew I could act. With the little time I had with Box-Head, I managed to rummage through its mind.'

'And... what do we do now?' he asked.

'I'm thinking, but listen, and I'll tell you what I've found out,' Rosemary began. She paused to catch her breath. 'Box-Head is a prisoner, it's stuck here. This is its sort of cell,' she waved her arms around in a circular motion and regretted it as pain resurfaced in her left arm.

'Are you alright?'

'It's just my arm after I fell back in the restroom. Listen, this whole forest is its prison. It's been trying to escape and it's almost succeeded.'

'A jailbreak?'

'Yes, a prison break.'

Scott threw his hands in the air, 'A jail, seriously? How can a prisoner have such a... it's a forest but you think it's an elaborate jail?'

'I only caught glimpses but...'

'Maybe I could listen and find out more like I did before...' Scott pressed his index finger to his temple.

Rosemary slapped it down with her good arm.

'Don't be stupid. You're not going anywhere near that creature. This is its territory and you're in no way ready for this! Good lord, I shouldn't have even brought you here.' She looked around hopelessly. 'What was I even thinking? They're right... all of them were right! I'm a stupid, old, woman who should have given up this caper years ago.'

'Well, you did and it's done. You had your reasons and now we're here so we need to get out of this place. You can give it all up when we get back.'

Scott began walking again.

'Box-Head's not strong,' Rosemary said following. 'That's why it brings its victims here from Euphoria. I don't think it can pass through the rift just yet. Box-Head's far too weak. But as its strength grows, it will eventually have the durability to pass through. Box-Head appears to be sick but nevertheless still deadly. I doubt it'll give up without a fight. It wants out. We have time as long as it doesn't feed.'

Scott slowed down allowing her to catch up. She pulled out a handkerchief and wiped her eye.

'And another thing, Box-Head's not working alone, someone at Euphoria has to be helping it.'

Scott raised his hand. 'Someone from the nightclub? From Euphoria? Who?'

'I'm not sure yet. There are over sixty staff. It could be any one of them,' replied Rosemary.

Scott threw his arms out. 'So, what do we do? How do we stop a... creature like this? If he gets to our world who do we call? The police? The army? They'll never believe any of this.'

Rosemary paced in front of him ignoring his question. And tapping her head several times. 'Think, woman, think! If I were Box-Head what would I do now? It's not strong enough just yet to use the rift but our presence here now...'

Scott took a deep breath. 'I'm guessing from your face that we haven't got much time?'

'Correct, time is of the essence, if by some unfortunate chance, Box-Head breaches the rift, its hunger will know no bounds. Once unleashed in our world its appetite will be uncontainable.'

Rosemary continued to pace and waved a hand dismissively in thought. 'Its companion, the fifth girl you encountered, she's now dead. It's still weak and possibly ill, so we may have some time.' She hesitated. 'I hope there's nothing too bad it can now do to us... but it's still got psychic and some telekinetic abilities. The women who were here didn't stand much of a chance against it. Our advantage is that Box-Head didn't expect to find people like us. We can defend ourselves, fight back.'

'How d'you mean?' Scott asked confused.

'It hadn't planned for people like us, paranormals, passing through the rift. Box-Head thinks mankind is weak, that we're easy victims. But it...' Rosemary pressed her lips together and her face looked pained.

'What's wrong?' Scott asked.

She slowly and quietly turned around on the spot. 'It's heading for the rift. That's what I'd do, regardless of how unprepared I was. This is what it's strived for.'

'What are you saying Rosemary?'

'I'm saying – us coming – you and me here to this place... Oh no! We need to get back to the monoliths and the rift now!'

'Why?'

'Trust me, Scott I'll explain as we walk,' Rosemary looked around. 'Buggar! Which direction? I think we're lost. I can't get my bearings.'

'It's this bloody mist and these floating crystal things,' Scott said. He grabbed at the flakes without success.

'Let's just head this way for now and trust our instincts.' Rosemary started walking. 'I've attempted to scan these flake structures, but they just dissolve on contact.'

Scott continued his futile attempts to catch a flake. 'Aren't they just snowflakes?'

'I don't think so. They look similar. A crystalline powder coming from above, falling through the atmosphere,' Rosemary locked eyes with Scott. 'I have an idea.'

'Shouldn't we get back to the monoliths first?'

'We will. Now help me.'

'What do you need me to do?'

'Find me a bit of space with not so many trees.'

'Are you 'avin a laugh?'

'You know what I mean.'

He looked around, then pointed. 'Maybe over there?'

Rosemary frowned and changed direction. 'Come on then and let's just hope Little Red Riding Hood doesn't come skipping through the forest at us – or worse some hulking great wolf.'

'I'm guessing I should maybe know what you're on about? What does that reference mean?'

Rosemary glanced at him sideways and shook her head. 'Seriously? Kids today don't even know the classics. Forget it, we have enough to do and time is not on our side.'

***

The mist cleared as Box-Head traversed the remaining distance and knelt beside the unnamed woman's lifeless form. She had been a companion of sorts and a valuable subject for examination. In her passing, she would continue to serve a purpose.

It applied pressure to various parts of her legs and torso. Tenderly, it supported the back of her head, tilting her face upward.

After a brief pause, it acted.

Box-Head drew the girl's knees toward her chest, enveloping her in its sinewy embrace. It inclined over her, delicately cradling her against its torso.

Now it would nourish itself and grow strong.

Once again, the eerie mist reappeared, descending like a silent shroud to envelope them both.

-32-

'What's the plan, Rosemary? You must have a plan. What are you thinking?'

'Yes, indeed,' she panted, taking hold of Scott's arm. 'Well, it's time. Time is somehow different here. It's not as set as I originally thought. Now we've been here a while I've noticed that we're most likely in a sort of pocket of time that's on a constant loop of a few seconds. When I first arrived here, a red maple leaf fell in front of me and vanished. Then a few seconds another one fell in the exact same place. Then, after you were taken by the woman, there was a flurry of these white flakes spinning in a certain pattern.'

'I saw the same thing now you mention it.' said Scott.

'I thought it was the breeze flowing through the trees on a current but now I know it was the same flakes in the same pattern repeating.'

'My brain hurts just listening to you,' Scott replied.

'Don't be silly. You're a smart lad, you're not daft.'

'I'm not too sure about that!'

'Anyway, back to what I was saying. It's like a vinyl record with a scratch. It keeps repeating. Please tell me you're old enough to remember vinyl?'

'No, I'm not,' Scott halted briefly before swiftly gesturing with his palms up. 'But I do know vinyl records and tapes.'

Rosemary stopped, placing a hand on her chest. 'How much further, Scott?'

'Just over there,' he waved towards some boulders in a less dense patch of trees where the ground rose higher. 'Carry on, what were you saying?'

'There is no time here. Not in the conventional sense, so nearly everything stays the same. The same gush of wind down the valley. The same maple leaf that falls but never reaches the ground. This is a prison set off in its very own pocket of time. Like a book set on a shelf or a pigeon hole in a pigeon loft.'

Scott guided Rosemary down onto a flat boulder.

'That's better. So what I'm thinking is that maybe nothing has changed here since the day Box-Head was brought in and locked up.'

Scott sat down on the grass, glad to be rid of the mist at this higher ground level. He glanced around for any signs of movement. 'Yeah, I understand that,' he sighed.

'If Box-Head was brought in here, then there must be an entry point, a doorway. The prison guards had to bring him inside.'

Scott rubbed his hands over his face. 'Not necessarily, he could have... I don't know... been beamed in?'

'You know Star Trek but not Little Red Riding Hood?' Rosemary grunted. 'One of the finer points of time is that you can enter in or out of it, either way, it leaves a weak point, a scar, a breakpoint.'

'And that's the cell door.'

'Exactly,' she shouted excitedly.

'So, where is this door?'

Rosemary raised an eyebrow at him. 'We're paranormals, look at our abilities, well mine. Do you remember what I can do that you cannot?'

He snapped his fingers and pointed at her. 'The vapour moth trail... thingy. You said you can see a person's movement within a certain environment.'

She nodded. 'A residual trail, where the person began in that environment and where they left, but only if I focus on that person or a tiny, localised area. Do you remember how Amy's residual trail led into the club's restroom and the cubicle at the end but it didn't come out or overlap?'

'Yes, but if you're thinking of doing it here... There are so many trees. Don't you need a clear path of vision or something?'

Rosemary placed a hand on Scott's arm. 'Help me up, son... ideally, yes, but it's not essential. I can give the trail light and structure allowing someone to follow it, which has proven very effective in the past. For me, it's like a tether line slightly pulling me towards it. It's my energy that reaches out towards that person's route.'

Rosemary narrowed her eyes and focused, a skill practised to perfection over many years. She saw the forest strewed out before her in her mind. Then little by little, she isolated parts in her mind, the shrines, clusters of maple trees, the monoliths and the Dolmen.

'I was in Box-Head's presence long enough to identify his unique signature.' She concentrated on as much of the forest as she could until she felt what she was looking for. 'There,' she pointed. 'And yes, we were heading in the wrong direction.'

Scott followed her finger through the trees. 'Let's go then. Do you need more rest?'

'No, luv, I'll manage. Our top priority is to find the anchor point for the rift at this end, it'll always be by the breach somewhere. We destroy it, preventing Box-Head from going through. follow me.'

-33-

Box-Head finally reached the grand circle of monoliths.

It had underestimated the older woman. Unlike the younger females, she did not carry a lifetime of negativity. Both she and the male possessed remarkable abilities, an unforeseen factor.

As the breeze blew by, it seemed to react, almost as if acknowledging him like an old acquaintance. However, in that momentary interaction, a poignant question lingered. Could this fleeting encounter with the repetitive gust be the final instance of such a familiar sensation?

It's focus snapped back to the two interlopers who had intruded on its realm, interrupting its plans for revenge. Its contemplations reverted to the imminent threat posed by these unusual and unexpected visitors.

In its observations of humanity, there had been nothing to suggest the human species had any unusual attributes.

Did its kin possess knowledge of these extraordinary individuals?

They knew and acknowledged the existence of humans, as recorded in historical texts, but the precise location of their world remained unknown. They merely knew of their existence, somewhere out there.

However, now it possessed a newfound awareness. It would amass strength and authority, ensuring its kin paid for the wrongs they had inflicted upon it. After meticulous planning, it could not risk jeopardising everything. Vengeance remained its driving force. Box-Head would bide its time, construct, and then return.

It squatted low, facing a peculiar assembly of small stones and twigs meticulously arranged on the ground. At first glance, it seemed like an insignificant arrangement, easily missed by a passerby. Yet, upon closer inspection, the stones revealed an unusual quality. Each one bore embedded citrine flecks, an anomaly adding an otherworldly gleam to the humble rocks. With a few deft adjustments to the design, Box-Head paused to concentrate. It extended its mental reach toward the male who had taken the life of its young companion. Beyond the rift, it had only encountered one other human male, but this one here was distinct.

Delving deeper into the young, unguarded mind, Box-Head unearthed something that instilled confidence within it.

The ebony monolith radiated a brilliant white energy. Box-Head stood at the threshold of the rift, infused with newfound vigour. It seemed attuned to the surges of bitterness coursing from the realm beyond, a realm it was poised to traverse.

The moment of truth had arrived.

Rising to its full height, the box held high, it seemed guided by invisible sentinels as it confidently strode into the luminous expanse with a sigh of contentment.

Then it was gone.

As the radiance waned, the huddled form of a woman materialised on the grassy expanse behind the monolith.

***

They had walked for a considerable amount of time before the ground started to rise. Up ahead a beautiful trail of emerald wisps appeared. They floated in a line, gentle, serene and magical.

'Your residual trail, I presume?'

'That's it, luv, but wait a second, we're... Oh my, I wasn't expecting it to be here!'

They came out from the trees and above the mist and onto the grassy ridge. In front of them stood the huge monoliths and to their right the Dolmen.

'We're... Oh dear! This is the same place we entered through the rift. I thought you were trying to find the prison door?' Scott asked and looked at Rosemary.

'I was... Now I see– of course! Look, look, look, where the residual trail originates from... it's the Dolmen? Now it makes sense. When we first came through, I scanned the Dolmen while you were passed out. I knew something was unusual about it.'

'The prison entrance to this vast forest is the Dolmen?' Scott asked.

'Yes, Box-Head's signature trail begins there and appears to pass by where you stumbled and lost consciousness. Its trail begins to fade down there amongst the trees... after,' she counted softly, '...five, six, seven... bingo! The trail from the Dolmen is roughly seven seconds.'

Scott stared across at her. 'Seven seconds? The loop is seven seconds long and then time... resets?' Scott rubbed both hands across his face and took a deep breath, 'Have I got this right? We're in a prison cell locked in a loop of seven seconds?'

He watched her as she examined the pockets in her jacket as if it were the most normal of conversations to have.

'Yes, simple really,' Rosemary replied retrieving her handkerchief. 'Very efficient. Imagine the number of prisoners you could lock up in say... hmm, ten minutes.'

'Then why aren't *we* looping every seven seconds?' Scott asked.

Rosemary wiped her eye and returned her handkerchief to her pocket.

'Not entirely sure. She replied. 'Some spirit and nether realms have unusual physical laws. We have entered an environment held in seven seconds. We are not part of the time freeze itself. The closest thing I know to this is environmental stasis. Each part of an environment is grown or manufactured, then held in its individual little bubble. After that, it's placed like furniture in a room. This whole valley of maples is an artificially constructed room – real trees held in their freeze-vacuumed pocket of time. A cluster of leaves falling repeatedly in the same pattern over seven seconds. Whoever they are, they have gone to a whole lot of trouble to create an environment for this Box-Head.'

'One thing has been bothering me,' Scott asked. 'How did they get hold of maple trees?'. 'They come from our world. Wait! Don't tell me maple trees are alien?'

'Don't be silly, obviously not. Well... I don't think so anyway. I don't know how they got here.'

'I still think I'm dreaming. I'm gonna wake up soon. So, we know where Box-Head was brought into his prison cell, so now what do we do?'

Rosemary walked toward the Dolmen 'Well, it's a prison, isn't it? Let's call the guards!'

-34-

The cubicle pulsed, brighter than ever.

Dan had not seen it do this before but then he had never known it to take three people in such quick succession.

He leaned on the sink and caught his breath. Tentatively, he picked up the needle and syringe and tossed them into the yellow plastic tub. He felt for the gun in his inside pocket, glad he hadn't had to use it. All he had to do now was wait for the rift to close as usual, seal the tub, throw everything in his backpack and then he was done. Get the hell out, report in and wait for the money to be transferred into his bank account. Not long now, not long at all.

He stretched his neck from side to side as he washed his hands, needing to remove any trace of the drug. The water was taking time to warm up. He caught his reflection in the mirror and exhaled.

'Wait! What was that?'

'I leave a trail because you're blind...'

The voice came to him like a whisper in the dark. Like the touch of a fly landing on a bare arm or neck. He spun around.

'I have waited for this most auspicious moment. You, who first heard my voice through the breach. The one who stabilised the link. The one who knew the honoured necessity of nourishing his god. I come now, to you, to your world, to make it mine. Come! Be with me, for I am now here.'

His blood turn to ice. He had only ever heard the voice in his mind. It had instructed him, promised to guide him and offered so much. From that first voice, he thought he was going mad, casting the blame on too much weed, drink and work stress. But the voice was now clear like he was hearing it from behind him.

Eyes wide, Dan stared, mesmerized as a colossal figure appeared in the light.

He stumbled backwards.

'I left a trail because you're blind. I place the leaves for you to find... me!'

Dan watched as the demon, its head cloaked in a cardboard box, materialised and crossed into the human world. Black claw-like hands appeared, wrapped around the cubicle doorframe. It held itself steady as it extracted its full body up through the light and into the cubicle that bowed under its elongated mass.

The demon wheezed and clicked like an insect as it tried to draw breath from beneath the wet cardboard box that covered its head.

Finally, it stood, its full height dwarfing the human.

Dan wanted to let out a cry, but the inside of his mouth lacked any moisture. His eyes were locked, fixed right back on the grotesque, gnarled body textured like a carapace. He had not expected this. Not to come through so soon, way too soon and not a demon like this.

Why hadn't they told him this might happen?

His thoughts went to his phone in the side pouch of his backpack, but he couldn't take his eyes off the noxious creature before him.

The demon's box tilted down to him. Slowly, it brought one long arm forward and Dan believed it would caress his head. But the arm began to twitch and shake, and the demon withdrew. The cardboard box moved in a manner that suggested awareness.

It was then that Dan knew the demon had opened a window into his mind. Across the distance of realms, all those months ago, he had felt this creature peer into his thoughts and heard it speak to him.

Everything had been so muddled and cloudy at first. The instructions were more like distant cries in a snowstorm. Dan felt that the demon saw all this and much more in his mind.

He knew the demon understood and felt his fear, revulsion, and most of all... betrayal.

Dan felt the demon delve into his consciousness, it sifted through fragmented recollections, like flipping through a family photo album. It witnessed the first time it had contacted him. Subsequently snippets of his past, moments that held weight in his brief existence. One vivid scene materialised – the first chilling encounter with the demon. Its plea for assistance echoed hauntingly in his mind,

...I need you. Help me.'

Another memory surfaced – men in dark sleek suits with green badges infiltrating his life.

...'You'll get your money, of course. Just do exactly what we say and that creature won't live to get through to our world...'

'Of course,' Dan replied and...

...Dan whooped with joy as the bank statement came through on his computer screen...

...received instructions, vials and syringes...

...'You're helping safeguard your country by doing this...'

The demon, having transversed the labyrinth of his mind, stood face-to-face with Dan. It knew the orchestrated plan to poison it and stop it breaching the rift into the realm of humanity, the very world it occupied.

'You conspired with others to kill me?' the demon hissed.

It was still in his mind.

Dan staggered back.

Should he make a run for the exit?

His bag was on the side near the creature. Everything that could incriminate him was in that backpack!

'I... I would never do that... everything I have done has been to help you!'

'You defile me with your lies. As base-in-nature as you are, you still attempt to deceive your god!'

The demon shook and wheezed. It brought its hand down on the backpack and hurled it behind. Then it came at him, spun him round and slammed him into a cubicle door. It grabbed him by the throat with moist skeletal fingers and began to squeeze.

Dan floundered, disoriented, as a giant sticky hand lifted him further off the floor. He fought against the panic and with his free hand pulled his gun from his pocket and fired.

Point-blank range.

And fired again.

The demon roared!

It knocked the gun away and Dan heard his own arm snap as if it was no more than a plastic straw. With one of the demon's hands constricting around his throat, he struggled until the pain overwhelmed him.

He screamed.

Two fingers from the demon's other hand became entwined, twisting together like a corkscrew locking together to form an eight-inch spike. It stabbed him.

A searing pain erupted within him, shock registering first, before agony engulfed his senses. His breath hitched, caught between a gasp and a cry. His eyes widened in disbelief, a fleeting moment of stark realisation.

The sensation of being forcefully propelled surged through him, His body launched across the room. He crashed mercilessly and slid across the floor.

Dan tasted metal in his mouth as he clutched his side, feeling the sharp sensation intensify. His whole body burned. It was not just the pain of being skewered like a pig or the broken arm, this was more. He drew quick breaths as he tried to ignore the numbness that quickly rose from his feet to his legs.

His fear appeared to subside. He would not die terrified. He had made something of himself, proven his family and teachers wrong. He was not a victim. Dan tried to laugh and spat blood.

'You... you think you can stay here... you're a dead man!' Dan screamed. 'You're half dead already. You stay and they'll – they'll hunt y – you down. The men you saw in the dark suits, they got technology and money, you filthy fucking shit! They don't want your kind here, none of us do. You torture me or kill me it makes no difference, you thick shit! They've been paying me to poison you for months! You're a dead man. Money, you hear me demon! Money, that's the only god that means anything in this world!'

The numbness rose to his head. Paralysed he sensed the creature over him, lifting him. It cradled him like a mother would a child in a gentle embrace. Dan was aware of the demon's chest beginning to open. He was being held tightly, so very tightly.

Amidst the swirling maelstrom of memories, Dan harboured a concealed smirk. An image surfaced, a syringe in his trembling hand, the contents ready to course through his veins. The recollection unfolded, the conversation with the shadowy men in sleek dark suits etched vividly in his mind.

...'You want me to inject myself with the same stuff I've given to the girls?'

'Yes, a full dose directly into the bloodstream, please,'

'A full dose? Are you insane? Just a safety precaution, you claim?'

'Yes, this modified dose will repel the creature.'

The reassurance offered no solace to his mounting fear. 'No! I'm not that fucking stupid!'

But promises of safety and more compensation echoed in his ears, a sinister melody, mingled with the gasp of disbelief as his eyes fixated on the digits of his bank statement...

Lies, lies, lies he knew that now.

...'Simply a precaution, just in case'...

In the waning moments before his unconscious mind seized his thoughts, a faint glimmer of clarity pierced through the haze. As the memories of his family, their faces, their laughter, began to fade in a distant mist, a chilling realisation unfurled within him. He was dying.

In his head, he screamed and the darkness closed in.

-35-

Rosemary withdrew the emerald residual trail energy back into her body. 'Something's changed, Scott!' She exclaimed spinning around to face the trees, monoliths and the Dolmen.

'What! What is it?' Scott asked a thrill of fear in his voice.

Rosemary closed her eyes. 'I'm struggling to sense Box-Head.'

'What do you mean?'

'I'm telling you, I think it's learned to block us!'

'Can it do that?'

'Apparently. I've been with it, stood in front of it. I know its signature. It's managed to shield its mind from me.'

'Rosemary, that means it could be near us! Getting ready to attack.'

'Yes, and there's something else... someone else, it's faint but there. Yes, yes, another signature. It's another person Scott, somewhere, somewhere close, someone new is here but it's very faint. Start looking for them!'

'Rosemary... what does all this mean? Please tell me what we are going to do?'

Rosemary walked back and placed her hand on his arm. 'We're going to find this other person, that's the first thing. Then find the mechanism that holds the rift open from this end and destroy it.'

'So Box-Head won't have any chance of getting through?'

'Yes, I'm not losing anyone else, Scott! Do you understand me? This new person is nearby– search the area around the monoliths and the edge of the trees they can't be far.'

She pushed Scott away and placed her hand over her mouth.

'What have I done?' she whispered.

A few minutes later Scott cried out.

'I've found her, she's here.'

Rosemary ran toward his voice. He was sitting behind the cracked dark monolith his arm around a dark-skinned woman no more than twenty years old. She wore cream wide-legged cargo trousers an orange openwork knit sweater and white trainers. Her eyes were closed.

'How's she doing?' Rosemary asked getting down.

'She's alive, unconscious I think, and she's cold I mean really cold. Maybe it's like what happened to me, you know passing out,' Scott said.

'Yes, more than likely. Here let me.' She placed her fingers gently on the woman's hands and listened.

Moments later, she let go.

'Her name is Jacqueline Bird, nineteen years old,' she murmured.

'How did she get here? Euphoria is closed. Did she follow us?' Scott asked. 'And wait a minute, I thought you weren't supposed to go searching in people's minds?'

'We aren't but there is a less-evasive level we can scan without going too deep, just to retrieve a few facts if the situation requires it. It's a fine line I know, I'll teach you it at some point. Now give her some time, her brain is attempting to re-set itself after the impact of the rift energy.'

She raised her hand, frowning as she wiggled her fingers. 'Weird, very weird. I've never been particularly good or speedy to access information through touch. Do you remember me telling you that? Psychometry has never been my strong suit, but suddenly I'm having no trouble at all.'

'Yeah, I remember you saying that. When you first put the leaf in my hand back at Euphoria.'

Rosemary shook her head and stood. She looked over at the Dolmen. 'Could it be that in this environment psychic abilities are enhanced?'

'Well, isn't that a good thing?' Scott replied, raising his eyebrows.

'Maybe, maybe not. Something Box-Head said to me. I've never known amplification of power to be a positive outcome in our line of work. Spirits sometimes take over a body causing a temporary increase in abilities. Other types of spirit energy can as well, but none of this should be happening here.'

She saw the way Scott was looking at her. She waved her hand. 'Don't worry, luv. Let's just focus on the task at hand and get us all back. We'll be safe on the other side. We can close and put a block on the other side, we'll figure it out.'

'Are we still going to alert the guards?' Scott asked.

'Yes luv, When we open the rift back we'll attempt to open the prison door. Hopefully, it's people will learn what it tried to do. We have to time it right, we can't allow its people to find the rift to our world. We need to open this dark monolith, then the Dolmen, pass through and close it from the other side somehow.' – She faked a smile. – 'I thought we could contain this, do it alone. But we must get back and get help.'

She watched Scott's jaw tense as he tried to wrap his head around what she was saying. Considering everything, he had handled things extremely well. She almost felt his frustration as he released his hold of Jacqueline and stood.

Scott indicated at the cracked darker monolith.

'Let's get this done, then we can get Jacqueline to a hospital?'

'Agreed,' Rosemary nodded. 'Let's find the mechanism that keeps the rift open from this end. I'm growing concerned about not encountering Box-Head yet but it must know our intentions by now.

'What type of mechanism are we looking for here?' Scott asked.

It'll be something out of the ordinary, a peculiar ritualistic assembly composed of elements from this ecosystem.'

They scoured the surroundings and Rosemary with her keen eye, eventually located it.

'Scott over here! This is what we're after,' she exclaimed pointing at the small stones and sticks arranged on the ground.

'I'd never have noticed this at first glance,' admitted Scott. But what do we do with it?' he asked.

'Gather up the rocks, especially the ones with the yellow flecks, they seem out of place in this ecosystem and are likely the key source,' Rosemary directed, beginning the task at hand. 'There all done. Box-Head won't be going anywhere. Time to open the rift. listen like I showed you.'

Scott, after clearing his throat and shutting his eyes, suddenly halted. 'Wait! How do I even begin to open a rift? I've gone blank?' He said, a note of concern in his words.

He heard Rosemary's voice. 'We're Paranormals, Scott, listeners. We access a spiritual library that allows us to seek information about things. You'll learn when you listen to whatever you focus on.'

'Like I did with the leaf?'

'Like you did with the leaf, yes, exactly. Now do it and then let's go home,' Rosemary commanded.

The ominous monolith stood before him.

Scott pulled his fingers through his hair. He took in a deep breath and fixed his gaze on the stones, their deep colours, textures and their shape. His breathing became calm. A surge of self-assured energy seemed to possess and take control of his body.

His eyelids closed.

Moments passed. His shoulders suddenly became hunched betraying the weight of some internal struggle. Fists clenched and unclenched.

An eerie white glow began to manifest but as suddenly as it appeared it faded.

The contours of his jaw tightened and then relaxed. His breathing quickened.

'Oh no, Shit! I can't do it,' he turned to her, 'I can't open it. Too much, it's all too much – I can't do it – I can't get us home! We're trapped!'

-36-

'It won't work. I don't know... I don't know how I did it before!' His voice had changed. No longer controlled and ordered, it was now full of fear. 'How will we get home?'

Rosemary returned to his side and lowered her voice. 'Scott, listen to my voice. How long have you been seeing Box-Head? How many nights have you woken up because it was part of your nightmares? I've seen it in your mind when you passed out after coming through the rift. I reached into your mind. I'm sorry I did it without permission, but I needed to know.'

'You did what?'

'The creature scares you, doesn't it? Answer the question, does it control you? Are you playing a game with me, Scott Finn?'

'No!' Scott snapped. 'I know what you're doing, but it's not enough. It's not going to be enough to open this bloody rift back home!'

'Of course, it is,' she snapped back. 'It's a door! But answer me this, what's that dark place, that impenetrable part in your mind? The one even I can't see past?'

'What are y – I don't know!'

'Liar! Does it know? Box-Head? Is that why you're here, Scott? Does it know what you're hiding? Is it something it needs or are you nothing more than a battery to be fed upon like the women it lured here? Do you know what that monster told me? It trembled with delight as each of those young women was dragged in front of it, petrified. They sobbed and wet themselves. They pleaded with it. They cried out for their mothers. They wanted to go home!'

'I don't know!'

'Yes, you do, Scott, tell me!'

'I don't know. There was an incident. I can't remember things I've done, people in my life!'

'And yet here we are. You, with this miraculous ability to open rifts to other worlds. Other planes with hardly any experience or practice! And that creature, that monster has been in your nightmares for – exactly how long have you been seeing it?'

'I told you; I had an accident back in February–'

'Maybe, Amy or Abby or all those women would still be alive if it weren't for you.'

Pure white light pulsed from the monolith. It increased and spread further, turning the monolith and the ground around it a brilliant white.

'What are you going to do?' Rosemary shouted back at Scott. 'What can you do? Will you do to me what you did to that woman in the shrine? What exactly did she see in you that made her throw herself off that balcony?'

'Stop it, Rosemary, stop it, right now!' Scott screamed.

'No! Tell me what she showed you?'

'She... she hinted at stuff, memories she could see. She said there were two of us, two sides to me and demons, wraiths, spirits, ghosts and sirens, jinns, artefacts, so many monsters, she saw them all in me. She said fucked-up things. It's not just her, it's my parents. They're like strangers, I don't recognise them when they look at me. They hate me!'

'They're your parents, Scott, how can you not know them?'

'The doctors called it a fugue state but my parents... I sense fear in them. I disgust them,' Scott screwed up his eyes. 'They won't talk to me about the incident, they lie and lie and lie. They stare at me when they think I can't see them. I think they stole my phone but told me that the police had taken it. Have I got any friends? Where are they? Surely, I had mates!'

Rosemary squinted 'Why don't you just ask them? Confront them? What's holding you back, Scott?'

'There's a feeling. It grows inside me. I don't want to face it. I don't want to know. I just want to be normal!' Scott staggered, eyes wide, tears streamed as he fell to his knees.

'You'll never be normal, Scott. Not now. You'll never have the answers you want because that creature, that monster is here somewhere with the potential to kill you, me! It will go through the rift, out through the cubicle at the end, then it is game over!'

'No! I won't let it,' sobbed Scott.

'We had the element of surprise before, but not now. It knows what I can do, what we can do and it'll be ready. Right now, we are the only thing that stands in its way, so it won't hold back. If it defeats us, it will feed off your resentment, your regret, and your frustration, gaining everything it needs.'

'No!'

'Remember how the rift had begun to expand at Euphoria? The collapse of that part of the nightclub will destabilise the rift. We'll be sealed here forever while Box-Head becomes strong and unstoppable! That's what happens if it gets through!'

'No!' Scott screamed.

He began to shake and rose back up. He raised his right hand towards the monolith. Light pulsed and grew brighter. It hummed like a generator.

He gritted his teeth as the light increased.

Rosemary stepped back covering her eyes as the rift appeared at its full intensity. 'That's it, lad, you've done it!

His shoulders drooped, and his face flushed, Scott wiped his eyes.

Without a word, Rosemary joined him. She placed her hand on his back. She hoped her touch conveyed understanding and empathy.

As the moments passed Scott breathed out steadily.

'You did that on purpose, didn't you? Did you honestly mean all that about me being in league with Box-Head?'

'No, luv. I think you know I don't really believe that. Now if you're ready, let's leave this place and make sure Box-Head is trapped here where it should be.'

'But the prison door, alerting the guards I couldn't open that door too it was just too much.'

'Let's count our blessings luv. It was a good idea at the time, at least we can get home.' She indicated for Scott to gather Jacqueline up and then guided them into the light. She gave a last look back at the haunting forest of red maples. 'Stay here and rot you monster.' She whispered and walked into the light.

-37-

Rosemary opened her eyes. She saw her reflection in the restroom mirror, her chest heaving and her clothes slightly dishevelled. Her radio and bag were on the sink where she had left them.

Blinking, she ran her hands over her chest and arms and let out a deep sigh of relief. Her shoulders, which had been held rigid with anxiety a few moments ago, were now relaxed.

Scott struggled to hold up a very limp Jacqueline.

'Are you alright, Scott? Keep hold of her... wait, you need to close the rift!' She snatched her bag and radio and frantically shifted them away from the cubicle.

'It's already closed, we're safe, we made it.' Scott stated.

With wide eyes, Rosemary glanced at the final cubicle, then swiftly back at Scott.

'Really? Good... Smashing!'

'What should we—'

Rosemary held up a hand to silence him and placed the radio back down on the sink. She took a moment to adjust her hair.

'But we did it Rosemary! The mechanism it uses... its gone, he can't hold open the rift from his end. We have these strange little stones of his.'

'No, no it's not that...I've failed Scott. What the hell was I thinking about bringing you into all this? I'm a stupid, stupid old woman, I should have listened to them. They said I was too old and I ignored them thinking I could continue like some reckless bloody teenager!'

Scott burdened by Jacqueline's weight, manoeuvred them both against a cubicle.

'Rosemary this isn't... I mean we...'

'Listen to me...The women are gone, Scott! If I had done something sooner, pressed harder on people I know. How can I face – Carol – little George – my friends knowing I could have prevented some of this?'

'Rosemary this isn't your fault. We didn't know how this was going to go down.'

She put her hands to her face. 'Didn't we? Isn't it all my fault when you really think about it?'

'No, it's absolutely something. Saving Jacqueline and preventing others from facing a fate with Box-Head is significant.'

She lowered her hands shaking her head.

And you... Scott, I brought you into all this and pushed you too far. I overstepped my role as an operant, all so I could get one more stupid adventure.' She began searching wildly through her bag. 'Where's my phone? I'm a stupid, stupid old – No, I've left it on charge at home – Scott, your phone...'

'In the van.'

'No!'

'Where is the nearest landline?'

'Manager's office, I think.'

Rosemary froze, her heart pounding in her chest. She couldn't tear her eyes from a pool of blood on the floor behind Scott. Questions swirled in her mind as a surge of dread washed over her. Scott pointed to a body behind him on the floor.

'No... Who?' she whispered.

'Dan...' Scott replied, 'and there's that.' He pointed to a gun on the floor next to a backpack.

'How? What happened, not Dan, please not him! Why would he be here and with a gun, for heaven's sake? Is he dead?' Rosemary asked.

'I think so.'

'Dan, what were you doing you foolish boy?'

'Maybe he knew about the rift?'

'No, no, no, something's not adding up here. Are we saying Dan was involved in this somehow, sending the women through the rift or going through himself?'

'I don't know. Or it's someone else and Dan found out and they shot him?'

'And leave the gun behind? I doubt it.'

'Do we take the gun?' Scott asked not knowing why he asked.

'No, leave it, fingerprints will be all over it unless it's been wiped clean. It'll be a shock for whoever finds him.'

'Do we just leave him here?'

'Yes, we need to get out of here and get help. They can't ignore my request for help now.'

'I've never seen a dead body before,' Scott replied.

'I know, luv, but try and put it out of your mind for now. I'll take the backpack on the floor over there with us. It's Dan's, I recognise it. It may give us some answers.'

She gestured for Scott to take Jacqueline out of the restroom. She retrieved her radio and put it in her bag. Carefully she manoeuvred around the blood and retrieved the backpack from the floor. Before she left Rosemary lightly lay a shaky hand on Dan's head and closed her eyes. Moments later she left the room.

Outside in the dimly lit corridor, Rosemary breathed out slowly. 'I'm removing evidence from a crime scene... I'm barmy.'

Scott suddenly began scanning the corridor, a flicker of unease tugging his senses.

Rosemary noticed the tension in his stance, a furrow forming on his brow. 'What's wrong?' she asked.

'I don't know,' Scott muttered, his voice barely audible. 'I just have this feeling like... like...' His voice trailed off, leaving an ominous void.

Rosemary's breath caught in her throat as she stepped back into the restroom, her eyes settling on Dan's bloodied body. Her pulse quickened, and she scanned the room she had cleaned so many times, her vision landing on the split door frame of the last cubicle as if some heavy weight had been placed upon it. It was an image that sent a shiver down her spine. Dread crept in as she attempted to dismiss the growing sense of foreboding. In a surge of panic, she extended her senses, hoping against hope that her fears were

171

unfounded. But the unsettling pieces fell into place, aligning with a terrifying truth she wanted to deny.

'It's here. Oh my God, it's here!'

Rosemary stepped back into the corridor and looked at Scott, her hands shaking.

'It's here,'

'Box-head?'

'It's here in the club. It made it through.'

'You said you couldn't sense him, it wasn't because he had blocked you....'

'It was because it had passed through the rift.'

Rosemary watched Scott's face contort in disbelief, his eyes widening in sheer shock as the horrifying truth sank in. She knew that look on his face, he had thought they had escaped, believed they were safe. But now she watched as the realisation crashed over him... somewhere in this very place, Box-Head lurked.

'Where exactly?' Scott's voice quivered.

'I don't know.' Rosemary's hand trembled as she ran it over her radio, frustration on her face. 'I told you I can't get an exact location on it and my radio is useless. I only know it's... it's here... somewhere, in Euphoria.'

'But the radio – useless?'

'EMF radios detect electromagnetic fields, but we're not dealing with a lost spirit or a possession.'

'Then let's just get the hell out of here and get Jacqueline to a hospital, call the Police, the army – somebody!'

'Can you carry her?'

'Have I got a choice?' Scott's tone wavered.

Rosemary clutched his arm desperately. 'Oh God, if it feeds!'

***

Maria Gilbert stared at the empty cardboard boxes strewn across the carpet just before the cellar door. What were they doing here? She walked down the corridor and glanced at the code lock securing her office door, prompting an eye roll. Left open again! Does no one care about security?

She pushed open the office door and strode inside flicking on the light switch and throwing a bunch of keys onto her already cluttered desk. Her coat fell onto a stack of boxes, all the while cursing under her breath. The handbag slammed onto her chair and she rummaged through it until her fingers found what she was looking for. With phone in hand, she leaned over to a wall panel, activating switches for the reception area and lower dance floor.

Leaving the office Maria made her way down the empty, quiet corridor, crossing over the dancefloor, and arriving at the reception and cloakroom area.

She tapped her fingers over her phone. After a pause held it up to her ear while checking the main doors.

'Voice mail!, why am I not surprised... Dan, I'm at Euphoria. Have you any idea why there's a fucking great big chain wrapped around the front door and empty delivery boxes left out over the ground floor corridor? Is this a joke?'

She pinched the bridge of her nose before continuing.

'I've had to come through the delivery gates and up through the cellar. Please tell me we have bolt cutters. Call me back... now!'

Stabbing a finger against the screen the phone found its place in her back pocket.

Exiting the reception area, Maria made her way to the lower bar, crossed the dancefloor and ascended into the DJ box.

'Let's get some music on because this place is giving me the creeps.'

She pressed several buttons, flicked switches and waited.
Nothing.
'Damn it!'

More buttons flicked, dials turned, her fingers running through her short black hair as she waited. Then the high-track lights illuminated, casting beams of coloured lights that danced around the dancefloor in absolute silence. Maria reached for the volume and the speakers hissed on with power. 'Why have I never learned to do this properly?'

Behind her, something huge and controlled descended in silence from the metal supports above. Black fingers uncoiled and wrapped around Maria's upper body like a child clasping a doll.

Maria screamed, pulling frantically at the relentless, clawed fingers that dug into her flesh.

Slowly, she was turned around and lifted, her legs flailing and body twisting. Above her, in the rotating-coloured lights, she saw the outline of a thin man-shaped figure. A cardboard box covering what would have been its head. The box moved casually around in the light.

Maria continued to scream until a large dark hand descended over her face.

'*Show me your life, Maria. The choices you did not make, the resentments, the failures, the missed opportunities.*'

She watched the creature in disbelief as it began to gently sway from side to side. Desperately struggling to break free, tears streamed from her eyes.

Then darkness rushed towards her as she felt herself lifted into the hidden depths of the room's vast ceiling.

Below the lights continued their silent dance, twisting and weaving across the empty dancefloor.

-38-

Screams echoed through the nightclub. Scott gently lowered Jacqueline to the corridor floor and Rosemary abruptly halted in her tracks.

'Someone else is here.' Rosemary closed her eyes. 'Another person is in the building. They must have not long arrived.'

Scott stood. 'It came from the lower floor, stay here with Jacqueline, don't move, I'll go.'

'Scott no! We can't split up it's too dangerous!'

He ignored her and ran down the rest of the corridor, running blindly, the only light coming from the emergency exit signs. Not considering the risk or even caring, he jumped down the carpeted stairs two at a time halting at the bottom to get his bearings.

Were those shifting colourful lights at the far end of the corridor coming from the dancefloor area?

He sprinted the distance.

Gulping for breath, he slowed as his feet hit the wood of the dancefloor. He took stock of his surroundings. Disco lights twisting, the hum of a sound system eagerly waiting for the introduction of music. The bar area with its lights from several well-stocked fridges offered a feeling of safety compared to where he now stood.

'Hello?'

He glanced into the dark seating areas of the room where the moving-coloured spots lights could not penetrate.

He stepped forward and cursed, realising he'd probably revealed his location.

Where had the scream come from?

A banging noise from above. He held his breath and looked up.

Nothing.

He suddenly felt vulnerable and small. The thought of finding the origin of the scream disappeared. He couldn't bring himself to continue the search. Scott retraced his steps back up to the first-floor corridor spooked enough now to whirl around at every shadow that moved.

When he reached the place, he had left Rosemary and Jacqueline there was no sign of them.

He ran the full length of the corridor and pushed on the emergency escape door at the end.

It rattled but it wouldn't open.

'Shit!'

His heart raced as he headed to the top floor, confusion mingled with growing concern. He dashed towards another door. However, his efforts proved futile once again as the second emergency escape door also stood firmly sealed, defying any attempt to budge it.

Each locked emergency door intensified the anxiety in his chest. He pounded on the barriers, mentally calling out for help.

Scott's heart skipped a beat at the unexpected sound of a voice in his head.

'Scott, follow my voice, come down to the first floor, we're along the corridor in the storeroom. Come quickly.'

The room was more like a cleaning cupboard than a general storeroom. It contained a sink, several shelves filled with cleaning products, boxes of blue paper towels, vacuums, mops, buckets and a cleaning trolley.

The fluorescent light of the room made Scott squint as he entered. The girl Jacqueline stood next to Rosemary with one hand on the sink and stared with dull brown eyes first at Rosemary then at him.

Scott stepped forward.

'I didn't find anyone. Someone was here though because the dancefloor lights have all been turned on.'

He saw Rosemary close her eyes and bring her hand to her mouth.

'Scott, oh lord. I can't sense them anymore, the person, they're... they're gone.'

'Maybe... maybe they just left?'

Jacqueline screamed and let go of the sink. She pushed herself away from Rosemary and staggered, crashing into the cleaning trolley.

'Wha... what? How did I get... she looked around like a deer in headlights. 'Please don't hurt me... please. I just want to go, let me go home!'

Rosemary stepped slowly towards her with her hands spread out.

'I know this is scary and what you've been through must be awful and very confusing right now but we three need to get out of this place and we need to go now.'

'W– where are we?' Jacqueline asked her hands shaking.

'You're in Euphoria the nightclub, you were brought here maybe against your will,' Scott said.

'Euphoria? This is Euphoria?' Jacqueline stammered. Her eyes widened with realisation, 'He drugged me. The fucking shit slipped me a roofie!'

'Calm down, you need to trust us, Jacqueline.' Rosemary stated loudly, 'We all need to get out of Euphoria as quickly as possible.'

'We can't,' Scott interjected.

'Why not?'

'All the doors... they're locked, even the fire exits... well on the ground floor, the one up here and on the floor above. I can't get any open, not one! That's not normal, is it? I mean the whole point is...'

'What do you mean the doors are all locked? We need to get out and call the police,' Jacqueline screamed. 'Are you saying we're trapped in here?' She staggered to the door. 'Where is my phone? Where's my stuff? Do any of you have a phone?'

Scott shook his head. Rosemary did the same.

'Fuck!'

Scott blocked her exit raising both hands. 'Let me go check the rest of the emergency escape doors on the floor above, but I have a feeling we'll find the same,' he glanced at Rosemary. 'I'll be right back.'

'Scott, wait!' Rosemary called. 'While you were gone, I found these in Dan's backpack. Syringes, needles and these small plastic bottles, one's empty. I scanned them, they contain a type of pathogen.'

Scott frowned. 'In English, Rosemary.'

'A virus, some sort of virus.'

'What for?'

'Hold on a minute... Box-Head said to me it had been poisoned.'

Scott pushed his hands through his hair. 'But that makes no sense, Dan poisoning Box-Head? He would have to have known things like this. And if Box-Head is here, why hasn't he just left the club?'

Rosemary turned away. 'Maybe it doesn't know how to. If it has been infected with a pathogen and subsequently passed through a dimensional rift in that weakened state... come on, Scott, you know the effect it had on you. We know nothing of its physiology. It may need time to recover. It can't just walk out onto the high street. At least here it...'

'Or he knows we can't get out so why kill us now when he can do it at his leisure.'

'Are you two insane?' Jacqueline shrieked. 'Can you hear yourselves? We need to get out and call the police I've been assaulted!'

'I'm sorry, Jacqueline, we'll find a way out but we need to do it safely,' Rosemary replied.

Jacqueline took a step back her eyes wide.

'How do you know my name? I never told you my name?'

In a sudden movement, she lunged ahead, shoving Scott aside as she sprinted out of the room.

A hand reached out to Scott as he turned.

'No Scott, let me go after her! Do what you said, check the upper floor and see if there's a way out, a window leading onto an emergency escape, anything.

'We need to get her back and stick together,' Scott replied pulling away, 'we don't know where Box-Head is.'

'I'm not leaving Jacqueline alone, Scott! Do you hear me? We've lost too much. Those women are dead. I won't fail this one as well. Box-Head is weak and we need to take advantage of that. We'll meet in Maria's office. That's the nearest phone.'

Scott's face fell, a heavy sigh escaping him as he shook his head in acceptance.

Rosemary closed her eyes. 'Jacqueline's heading for reception and the entrance. The young woman certainly knows her way around the nightclub.' She slipped Dan's backpack on and gripped her own bag tightly.

Scott nodded, raising both hands briefly before darting out the door.

***

'Shit!'

Jacqueline stumbled into a fire extinguisher. She regained her balance and commenced her careful but anxious walk over the dancefloor with spinning lights and into reception. She limped to the main doors, turned the smooth bronze-coloured lock clockwise until she heard the click and pulled.

Nothing happened.

She tried it repeatedly.

'No! No! No!' she screamed, 'open this door... the door's locked! Somebody please help me!' Jacqueline frantically rattled the large doors.

Rosemary came up behind her and grabbed her shoulder. 'You need to calm down and be quiet. I'm serious. We're in trouble and I need you to take control of yourself!'

'Let me out, let me out!' Jacqueline sagged against the wall and began to sob.

'Scott said it was locked,' said Rosemary releasing Jacqueline and placing her own hands flat on the door. She pushed a few times and heard a familiar clinking sound outside.

'I know a chained door when I hear it. We opened it when we first arrived and put the lock on from the inside.' Rosemary explained. 'So, someone wanted us trapped inside.'

'I don't care who locked the bloody door I just want to go home.' Jacqueline gasped for air.

Rosemary lowered herself down in front of her and took her hand.

'Please trust us, we are the best chance you have of getting out of here,' she whispered into the woman's ear. '*Step in the cave and keep cool.*' Her words flowed gently, familiar and reassuring, a concise sequence crafted to channel her energy and magic.

Moments later Jacqueline stopped crying and blinked her tears away.

'You know my name, but no one calls me Jacqueline, it's Jax, just Jax.'

'Well, Jax, we need to get out of here. If you come with me to the manager's office, we'll wait for my friend. There should be a phone there we'll call for help.

'If you try anything,' Jax said frowning.

'Yes, I'm sure I'll regret it,' Rosemary said winking at Jax.

Leaving reception, they crept silently past the bar. On their left, the dancefloor and its lights swirling around like phantoms.

A loud creaking resounded through the room. Rosemary spun around searching for the sound. She grabbed Jax and together they flattened themselves against the nearest wall. The disco lights danced in front of them. It was difficult to pinpoint where the noise came from. She closed her eyes and reached out into the visual confusion her heart beating loudly.

Another creak, closer this time.

Jax heard the sound now too.

'I think it's coming from the DJ box over there. I think it just moved,' Jax whispered.

'We need to go!' Rosemary said working out the distance to the corridor and Maria's office. 'Right now, Jax run!'

They began to run.

What was that?

Rosemary stopped, spun and screamed. A large black hand had wrapped around Jax's throat from behind. The creature unfolded its bulk from the corner of the bar, a new cardboard box adorned its head.

It rose like a demon from hell.

-39-

Jax struggled. She rose into the air, the creature holding her from behind.

'No! No! Leave her alone!' Rosemary screamed. 'Put her down!'

It ignored her plea and pushed one side of the cardboard box along Jax's thrashing head.

Jax made gurgling noises while grappling for breath. Her hands tugged frantically at the huge, interlocked fingers around her throat.

Rosemary heard a series of long deep inhalations from inside the box. It began swaying from left to right.

'No! No! Leave her alone, put her down,' echoed Box-Head, his voice low and calm, softened by the box.

'You're here. You made it through the rift. Put her down, you don't need to hurt her you've won!' pleaded Rosemary.

'Fascinating. Once again you stand before me. Armed with deception, nobility and human morality. Yet, you use your kind as vessels to poison me and prevent my release.'

Rosemary lunged forward and grabbed at Jax but it was no good.

Jax continued to squirm like a fish on a hook. Her eyes bulged. With a single twist, Box-Head threw Jax through the air across the dancefloor like a toy. She crashed to the ground sliding until her body smashed into the DJ booth.

Rosemary froze.

Box-Head began to circle her. Coloured lights moved across the cardboard and gleamed off its black carapace body.

'And all for nothing. I have fed on two since being in your world and I have tasted the sweetness of resentment and loss in all its purity. I grew stronger and more focused because of it. My path is still before me. But tell me, Rosemary, the empathy I felt in you... how could you use your kind in such a way as vessels to poison me? Could it be that we are not so different, after all?'

'I'm nothing like you,' Rosemary's shaking hands covered her neck and chest. 'Two? Did you say two? You've killed again? The man upstairs, Dan, next to the cubicle his body....'

'The male, Dan Blaine, he served me. He chose the females, sending them through the rift to me. I promised him much. He could have been a ruler over your crude cattle species but just like you, he chose betrayal.'

Rosemary balled her hands into fists and dropped them to her side.

'And the other?' The screams we heard?'

'Maria Gilbert. I have released them Rosemary, both from a life of distrust, control and misery. She is part of me now, how can you not want that for those who are sad, weak and lost.'

Rosemary froze. 'Maria, no....'

The box tilted.

'Once more you attempt to deceive, stating that you care. I have been in your mind, Rosemary Moon. I saw and felt that you were genuine in this misguided emotion called empathy. Yet your behaviour, your very actions betray you. Tell me, how do you accomplish this? I intend to understand all aspects of the human psyche. Why did you saturate the last females, Amy, Nadine, Gemma, and now this one with poison? Your species have so many colourful ways of destroying things you do not understand?' A crooked finger pointed to Jax's motionless body. *'It seems so unlike you to adopt such a heinous strategy.'*

Rosemary shook her head and her shoulders fell.

'We haven't done anything. I... I haven't been poisoning you.' She spread her hands out in submission and stepped back, her mouth open and her eyes wide.

'You liar! Your abhorrent kind has infected me on the orders of the men in grey,' Box-Head yelled.

'I know nothing about men in grey and their orders. I came to you! I gave you a choice to stop what you were doing with the offer that we help you find another way. Don't be so blind! Why would I present that to you if it was secretly infecting you?'

Box-Head swayed in the lights like a shadowy pendulum.

'What are you waiting for?' Rosemary shouted. 'Why don't you just leave? Leave this place go on, get out! You've found a less rancid box to cover your head, I see, so why not leave?'

'Maybe, I am unsure how to do so. This environment is sealed, it is strange to me. Why should I leave when all I have to do... is wait.'

'Wait... wait for what?'

'For you to bring me exactly what I need!'

Rosemary stopped her retreat.

'Scott!' whispered Rosemary.

A figure came out of the darkness behind Box-Head launching himself up, swinging a fire extinguisher like a hammer. It slammed into Box-Head's side, the same site where Dan had shot it at point black range.

Box-Head's roar filled the nightclub. It crashed to the floor.

Scott dropped the fire extinguisher, spotting the word 'Phaedrus' written upon it. Dismissing it, he stumbled over to Rosemary. 'Are you okay? Where's Jax?'

'Over here.' Rosemary ran over the dancefloor to where Jax lay. She got down, placing her hand on the young woman and closing her eyes. 'She's alive but unconscious. Help me put her in the recovery position. We'll have to leave her here.'

'Leave her here? Are you crazy? She's defenceless.'

'We have no choice. She's no threat to Box-Head and she's likely filled with that drug Dan gave her.'

'What are you on about?'

'Scott, we need to go. Quickly get to the manager's office, it's you! It's you it's after!' She got up. 'Scott, what are you doing, get away from it!'

He just stood staring at the huge writhing black creature on the floor with a cardboard box for a head.

'Scott!' Rosemary snapped. 'Now!'

He took a step towards the hideous creature bathed in floating lights.

184

'You. It's *really* you,' Scott growled. 'In my nightmares, in my head, all this time. At some point, I thought you were made up.'

Rosemary moved between Scott and the creature.

'Enough!' She screamed. 'Move away, Scott! Something isn't right, it's playing with us I can feel it. It got out, it achieved its goal, why stay here? What happened? It said it's waiting fo –' A look of confusion crossed her face as she glanced at a dark fluid spreading across the floor in the lights.

"What's the smell?' Scott covered his mouth.

'Is that blood coming from it? Tell me if I'm wrong, Scott?'

Scott stood motionless.

'I couldn't have done that much damage to it. It felt like I was hitting a brick wall,' Scott muttered.

Rosemary took his arm, 'The gun, the gun Dan had. Maybe he shot Box-Head? Scott, are you listening to me?'

Sweat broke upon his forehead. Like an automated robot, he turned to Rosemary. His chest rose, his breath a rasp in his chest. He raised an eyebrow.

Rosemary's face clouded and he understood.

'Why not?' Scott gasped. 'You said it's weak possibly shot. How weak is it?'

'I've no idea, but it killed Dan and fed off him and then Maria. In the restroom, after you and Jax left, I had time to scan his body. It had the same chemical signature as the liquid in the bottles with the syringes. Box-Head needed the women, their resentment and regret. That creature has taken five women,' she put her hand to her face to hide her features. 'Five beautiful young women.'

'It's killed Maria? The manager? Then let's kill it. Just kill it!'

Rosemary's eyes widened 'We don't do that, Scott, I don't do that!' She snapped. 'Leave it. It wants you.' Rosemary pulled him away. 'Maria's dead, yes, maybe she was laced with the drug too, which means it may have had a powerful dose in a short period. We still have a chance to get out. Maria must have gotten into the club some other way.' She touched his bare hand.

'Are you sure?' Scott asked a sudden calm flowing through him.'

'She would have gone straight to her office.'

Their gazes momentarily went to Jax and then they turned and ran.

Reaching the office, Rosemary frowned at the open door and the light coming from it. She glanced at the door's entry keypad before entering. The Venetian-style blinds were closed and the walls were lined with more boxes which made the room even smaller.

'Hold on a minute, Scott. We need to destroy any evidence that we were here. Grab the VHS tapes. Always hide your tracks lad.' She crept over to a large door at the back with a chrome keypad to the side.

'Someone has already entered the code. The door is open.'

Inside the small cupboard, she quickly scanned the dials and monitors. 'It's not working, the CCTV, none of it. It's always on whether the club is open or closed, especially after what's been going on, but it's all switched off.'

She locked eyes with Scott.

'Dan must have deactivated the whole system so as not to incriminate himself.'

There was a coat thrown over the boxes across one wall and a handbag on the nearest chair. Rosemary quickly rummaged through and pulled out a hairbrush. 'I need something of Maria's so I can locate her residual echo. I'll be able to exactly see where she entered.' She edged around the cluttered room scanning the desk, finally snatching up a set of keys.

'Rosemary, you said Box-Head wants me. What does it want?'

'I'm not entirely sure but it appears we're not the only ones who didn't want Box-Head to come here through the rift. There's a second group involved.'

'A second group? Who? People like you – I mean us?'

'No not Paranormals, not like us. Men in grey suits and green emblems. Anyway, I have what I need.' She jingled the keys. 'Let's do this. The only problem is... we need time to do it. Scott keep a look out for Box-Head, it can only come from the dancefloor down this corridor,' Rosemary explained.

She felt Scott's hand on her arm.

'Back there, I wanted to kill Box-Head, I just felt a surge of anger and what I did back in the forest, in that barn to that... that woman.'

'It's okay, luv, I know – I saw what you did. I felt it too, I guess after confronting that – look... let's find a way out of this place and get help. There are organisations out there that can't ignore me, not now. This is beyond us. I have a daughter, a grandson and a world I want to keep safe. I'll be damned if a scrawny box-headed psychopath is going to take them all from me. I'm sure you have people you love,' she smiled reassuringly.

Scott just nodded 'According to people who knew me before I've wasted my life. I've fucked things with my family. I'll find you the time you need to locate Maria's trail.'

He ran back out of the office.

'What? No! Scott, wait!'

-40-

With little thought for his safety, Scott ran back to the dancefloor. There he stood beneath the dancing-coloured lights. Box-Head was gone.

Jax was there. He checked her breathing before returning to the spot where Box-Head had fallen. He bent down and pulled his fingers through a dark liquid on the floor.

He stood wiping his fingers on his jeans and crept over to the bar. He edged around it. Passing through the bar hatch he peered into the illuminated fridges. Why were the fridges so curiously intriguing? An irresistible yearning pulled at him, despite his initial intent to create a distraction, which now evaporated like a dream upon waking.

A myriad of bottles in various hues of green and brown neatly lined the shelves. He slowly backed away from the glass his stomach muscles tightening, his eyes wide. Every label on every bottle read 'Phaedrus'. Phaedrus lite, Phaedrus mild, Phaedrus cider. Even the mixers and fruit juice cartons displayed the singular word in different fonts. His gaze darted across to the glass shelves twinkling in the lights and to the bottled wines lining them. Eyes drifted up to the optics hanging down ready to dispense their designated measures.

His heart missed a beat.

Where were the Shiraz, Merlot, and Rioja? All bottles were instead labelled with the word Phaedrus. And there was Phaedrus vodka, Phaedrus rum, Phaedrus whisky, Phaedrus gin. His lower back hit the bar with a dull thump. This is ridiculous. This couldn't be right. Am I going mad? He spun round and placed his spread hands flat on the bar counter. He dragged them along the surface forcing his legs to walk. Got to get to the room behind the bar. Once inside, he stood against a wall as if trying to avoid being seen. He breathed out. The room was dark except for a tiny red light indicating a glass washing machine.

That word again... that fucking word, it's real it has to mean something.

Scott breathed out again this time more slowly. He needed to calm down. All the crazy events he had been through recently... why would this one word be so unnerving and haunting to him?

Being overtly aware of the question gave him the answer instantaneously. The happenings that had transpired were all external; the rift, the forest and even the confrontation with the feral woman to a large extent were tangible. They were tied to the external world and so could be dealt with physically. This one-word, Phaedrus was personal, internal, deep as an abyss and part of his unconscious, an unconscious that no longer wished to remain so.

'I can do this. I can do this,' he whispered.

He returned to the bar, his nails digging into the palms of his hands.

Looking again at the refrigerators and the optics, he took a single bottle from the shelf. 'Merlot,' he turned the bottle around in his hands. He replaced it and took another, 'Shiraz,' then another...The word Phaedrus had vanished, The labels were back to their usual branding. He backed out through the bar hatch.

A shadow fell over him. He gasped, and spun, finding a dark shape disentangling itself from the darkness above.

'Oh no—'

'Oh no—' Box-Head echoed its box jerking sharply from left to right.

'Hello, Scott — Hello Scott — Hello Scott.'

After a final shudder, the box ceased to move.

'Scott,' the voice was deep, calm and almost perfectly human. *'Not how I imagined our first meeting. But let me begin by saying, I will very much need you if I am to remain here.'*

It reached out its long arm and uncurled its fingers which clicked like wood consumed by fire.

'Go to hell!' Scott whispered.

Scott felt a malign pull like a magnetic force. This was the same sensation from the nightmares! The same as in the restroom with the cubicle door!

'*I'm in your head, I'm in your mind and unlike Rosemary, it would appear you have neither the experience nor power to stop me.*'

Scott felt as if ice had penetrated his body.

'*Scott, let me pull back the veil in your mind. Let me give you a gift, a gift of your true self, but first...*'

Scott watched in horror as his right arm lifted and waved from left to right.

'Go... to... hell!' Scott repeated. 'Let me go – what do you want from me?'

'*Fascinating. Here I thought Rosemary was the curious oddity. A being as small and insignificant as she, holding such a strong desire to care. A strong empathy for one's fellow kin and yet here you are, a male who does very little in the way of care. Where is Rosemary hiding? Does she flee, unlike you? If only I'd had the strength to reach out sooner, pull you through and absorb your hidden remorse and suffering.*'

Black spine-like fingers clicked and twitched. It waved them slowly in front of his face.

'*Arrrh, unlike Rosemary, I see you are unable to prevent my paralysis, yet there is so much untapped power in you. So much hidden darkness. Once uncovered, think of the anger, resentment, self-loathing and disgust within you, so ripe and dripping with sweet purity.*'

Fingers clicked faster and faster; a chattering sound came from deep within the box.

'*And to imagine all this time you were there at the edges of my consciousness when I reached out beyond my forest. You with the power to open pathways to different realities. Scott, we, the Shroud, are a most resilient species.*'

The chattering sound ceased, replaced with a deep wheezing from beneath the box. Slowly, it moved from side to side in a figure of eight.

'*You will not defeat me. You have already lost. You and only you, Scott, have brought me the means to grow and to finally return to seek revenge on my people. To deliver them onto the righteous path.*'

Scott felt himself lifted into the air. He floated forward.

'This excites me,' Box-Head hissed. *'I will rip through into your mind and uncover this darkness and devour it, but you will remain alive.'*

Box-Head's wheezing was now sickening; droplets of black liquid spattered from beneath the box, but it did not stop. Menacingly, it remained standing in front of Scott.

The voice of Box-Head resonated in Scott's head laboured and breathless with an undertone, an edge, an unsettling harshness.

'Show me your missed opportunities. Share with me your life, Scott. The ungrateful son, the boy who turned to opiates, stimulants and sedatives. He who sold them to the sad, the depressed, the weak. The man who fell into despair, stole from his parents and watched them struggle to keep their home. Arrr, what is this...' Box-Head paused then began to nod. *'Guilt... so much culpability. A dark-haired woman... fighting, yes, fighting repeatedly for your affections. Rejected to the point of despair. Driven to take the drugs you sold, all on the chance you would notice her. Now she is... dead! Dead because of you, Scott Finn! Because of your reprehensible life. Yet another of your species saturated in misdirected love for a lost ruinous soul.'*

Scott's bottom lip trembled. Tears ran down his face and his throat tightened. It was all true and it all flooded back in one vast, crushing deluge.

'Exhilarating, wonderful, arousing! Your emotions appear to be pushing you past my paralysis. Emotions so rich, so succulent, this is the key to your power, Scott.'

Fibrous arms he couldn't feel wrapped around his chest and back. The cardboard box tilted to one side.

'Let me rip back... the final hidden barrier. Then I will feed and then—'

Silence.

The voice in Scott's head was gone.

Scott stared ahead. A sense of awareness crept into his mind followed by a split second of unity and peace.

Box-Head's movements abruptly ceased. Its body flew backwards through the beams of light, crashing to the floor at the base of a wall. It screamed, struggling to rise, its legs contorted. It collapsed back to the floor. The grating howl rose, it resonated around the dancefloor a chilling sound that would make any blood run cold.

Scott could feel once more. The invisible force faded. Instinct took over. He fell into a crouching position and gasped for air.

'I have to thank you,' Scott coughed, 'Seriously, I couldn't remember... Oh God, it's all coming back! I was... I almost destroyed my parents. I hurt people. The drugs, the drink. Self-hate, too deep, too lost. Oh god, no! People who loved me, Mom, Dad. I should have asked for help.

Scott stood and staggered.

'A young woman.' Scott's eyes went wide. 'She loved me, saw more in me... Oh no. No, no, no. She wanted to get me away from the drugs. I was evil to her. Too greedy, too selfish. She went and... she died. She died. I was there.' His voice raised an octave. 'She died because of me.'

Gripping his chest, he stepped forward.

'For god's sake, I was the monster! Me! How – how could I have been that type of guy? How many other lives have I destroyed?

His head cocked to one side. He considered the creature splayed out before him and ran his hands over his face.

'I have to live with that. I now have a choice. That was the man I was, but not the man I chose to be. The man who stands before you is Scott Jacob Finn, and I will not be controlled by you. I will not be controlled by anyone!'

A voice called out. Scott spun around, searching for the source. A voice came again but realised it was only in his mind. The voice became an invitation. He rubbed his temples. It was that feeling again. The one he experienced after leaving the shrine in the forest. He spun quickly to face the main corridor leading to the upper floors.

There it was again.

He observed Box-Head's struggle on the ground, attempting to rise. Despite its efforts, its legs faltered, a guttural howl escaped and it collapsed once more. But within moments Scott saw its body steady, the trembling in its limbs ceased, and strength visibly surged back into its form.

'Screw this,' Scott muttered retreating backwards from Box-Head and off the dancefloor. The invitation in his head still urging him on.

'Rosemary.'

He ran.

-41-

Euphoria's kitchen had been installed well. Extraction systems, food preparation areas, storage, hot cupboards and gantries, all in commercial-grade stainless steel. Rosemary stood at the dishwasher table looking up at a clock. She jumped as Scott burst through the door.

'Scott! Oh, thank the lord!'

She ran and wrapped her arm around him.

'I was so worried, you stupid boy! Are you alright?' She let go and stood back.

'Just got done – running – was – was that you in my head showing me – showing me you were here?' Scott asked panting, leaning over, hands on his thighs.'

'Yes, like I did back in the forest, remember?'

He waved a palm at her. 'Hold on a minute, why didn't you just use telepathy?'

'Wha... what?' Rosemary's eyes widened.

'Paranormals have telepathy, why didn't you just say Scotty come to the kitchen?'

'How do you know about telepathy? I was holding off on that till – wait... just wait, it's not important! Look, look, I've found out how Maria entered Euphoria. It was through the cellar and up that chute with the hatch where the beer barrels get delivered. We can get Jax and leave right now!'

'No, no, we can't,' Scott replied.

Scott climbed up onto a food preparation table and started messing with something high up on the wall.

'Jax is still unconscious,' he said. 'If Boxy was able to feed on her regret, then he would have done it by now. She's safe for the time being. I've just met Box-Head and what he wants or... what it wanted because I guess it's all irrelevant now – was my so-called darkness. All that stuff I couldn't remember following the fugue.'

'Er, yes, of course, I remember.'

'There's also my power to open rifts.'

He jumped down with something in his hand.

Rosemary stood mouth open, 'Wait! You confronted Box-Head? How did you get away? What's happened? You... You sound different, your voice – words?'

Tears escaped Scott's eyes. He took a step towards her and she felt a hand on her arm.

'Have we the time? Box-Head will be coming. Rosemary I want you to reach into my mind and scan me. The way you did back at the monolith..'

Without question, she reached out and placed a hand on his cheek. She closed her eyes.

Rosemary found herself on a grassy bank, looking over a caravan site. Scott was at her side.

The sky was overcast and cold, and the sound of children drifted on a breeze.

She blinked a few times. Scott turned away and she joined him.

A meandering stream chuckled happily and sprawled out on the grass was a figure, unmoving, pale and dishevelled.

'Is that–'

'Yes, Rosemary, that's me,' Scott said.

'I don't understand?'

'This is the day. The day I tried to take my life.'

'What?'

'I remember... throwing my wallet, my phone, everything that had any record of me into a rubbish bin at the train station.'

'Oh, luv...'

'Next thing I know, I wake up here on this bank, no memory of who I was or how I got here.'

'Some... perhaps something inside you didn't want you to take your own life.'

'I guess. The fugue erased my mind. The guilt, shame, the depression. I just didn't want to go on living anymore. The fugue saved me, it–'

'– a part of you wanted to go on living, Scott.'

'Yeah, that would make sense.'

Scott manoeuvred around his body and got down onto the grass.

'Take a look at this bottle, not the beer bottle, the other one, this blue one.'

She joined Scott and examined the blue bottle in the grass.

'Interesting...'

'It's a weird bottle, why would I be holding it?'

'I don't believe it weird! It's similar... to my witch bottle at home. Did you know this? It's a little bit different but it's definitely a type of witch bottle, you can make out the ornate glass and the marking under all the stains and dirt.'

'And in your experience, Rosemary, what are they generally used for?'

'Based on what I'm seeing I would argue it's a vessel for holding a spirit, or possibly an entity.'

'Rosemary, I'm holding it in my hand. If I have it in my hand, where did it come from?'

'The stream... Look at the algae encrusted on it. It's chipped and scratched and the discolouration of the glass shows severe weathering. I would guess it's been in the water for a very long time. Scott, do you still have this bottle?'

'I don't know, I don't think so.'

'If you still have the bottle, we can scan it and obtain its history, everything about it.'

'Oh, yes of course. I'm not sure what I did with it but I do remember that I opened it.'

'You opened it... and what happened?'

'Phaedrus, his spirit, psyche and... his memories.'

'They came out?'

'Yes.'

'Like a Genie out of a bottle.'

'Yes, but that Genie entered me, Rosemary, entered my mind, curled itself up deep in my unconscious.'

'And...'

'...and that's where it's been... till now.'

'Are you saying this Phaedrus has possessed you? Is it inside your mind now? Is it benevolent?'

'I believe so.'

'None of this makes any sense Scott.'

'It will Rosemary, it will. I think he's one of us. Phaedrus was one of us.'

'One of us?'

'Yes! Yes! Rosemary, he's like us.'

'What do you mean? A paranormal? Is that what you mean?'

'Yes, I think he is– I mean... was.'

The scene washed away.

They now appeared on a cliff top. The sun was beginning to set. Shades of orange, pink and purple creating a stunning vista, with the last remaining rays of sunlight casting long shadows across the land.

Scott stood tall and a more imposing figure it seemed, with arms crossed and eyes fixed on the horizon. Strands of his dark hair swept gently across his face and his military green jacket fluttered slightly in the sea breeze.

His eyes were drawn to the cemetery below, which overlooked the sea. Despite the eerie location, Scott radiated a sense of calm and tranquillity that seemed to permeate the entire area.

A lone seagull cried out its piercing call bringing Scott out of his moment of unity. He unfolded his arms and walked over to a weathered wooden post with three signs giving directions: *Coastal path... Mortehoe 1.2 miles.... Morte Pointe 0.5 miles.* He lightly drew his fingers down the wood and then turned to her.

'I've seen this before.'

She didn't answer she merely tilted her head as Scott looked across at the cemetery.

'Are you alright, Scott?'

'Yes, but I've seen all this in a dream, I just thought it was made up.'

'So, you've seen this exact place. Where is it? It looks like Cornwall maybe Devon?'

'It's Devon... I know that. This is where it happened. It's all coming back. This is where Phaedrus fell.'

'Fell?'

'No, not fell– ended– this is where he was cursed. A spell cast with strong intention by a being, an evil that Phaedrus fought. He defeated it but in the last moments before its confinement, the darkness–.'

White light erupted from Scott's body and a guttural voice resonated throughout the sky.

'Hear ye, in imprisoning me, thou shalt incarcerate thee, I doth take from thee, Phaedrus Castellanos, all that thou art and all that thou might haveth been, yea, even thy past and thy very future. I doth curse thee to wander aimlessly in the void, lost in time never to behold a past nor a future, a mere shell, a shadow on the street corner, a cry in the vast ocean. Until thou vessel is uncovered by one equally devoid of remembrance... thy body shall remain as vacant as solitude itself.'

The illumination around Scott faded like a dying ember gradually diminishing until there was nothing but a soft white glow around Scott's hands. The silence was discernible, broken only by the soft whisper of the wind as it carried the last strands of white away.

Rosemary took Scott's hand. 'Scott... do you know what this means? This means it was you. Fate or destiny, it doesn't matter. You broke the curse, you have the memories and experiences of this man, Phaedrus, this paranormal, one of us.'

In the fading light of dusk, Scott and Rosemary stood silently on the cliff gazing out at the cemetery below, lost in their thoughts.

The scene washed away.

She opened her eyes and blinked.

'If Box-Head absorbs you,' Rosemary cautioned, 'it'll acquire all of Phaedrus, becoming unstoppable.'

'I am aware,' Scott acknowledged, lifting a wall clock to his face. 'But I have a plan!'

-42-

Holding Dan's backpack firmly with both hands, Rosemary reached Jax on the dance floor unopposed. She got down and lay a hand on the young woman's head.

It was difficult to think straight.

Only metres away was the outside world and help. Would it be more sensible to leave?

No, I'm not leaving Jax here any longer, not like this, not undefended, she thought.

The dancefloor felt eerie. How empty and lonely the club was with only the hum of a speaker system, dark alcoves, hypnotic lasers, strobes and moving heads dancing to silence. The cleaning shifts were always full of music and smells of coffee, bacon and egg sandwiches.

She glanced back down at Jax and images of Carol and George came to mind. George would be asleep and Carol would be watching some police drama by now. How normal that seemed.

Take a deep breath, Rosemary.

What was that?

She held her breath.

The sound came from above like someone knocking into pipes. She rose and stepped slowly back across the dancefloor.

Is that creaking up there?

The lighting walkways, there's something up there.

'Scott? Scott is that you?'

Silence.

Rosemary continued walking until she reached the bar counter a few steps ahead. The refrigerator lights offered comfort. She kept her back against the counter, her face beaded with sweat.

Where do I look?

She took a few tiny sidesteps towards the corridor.

Something moved again up in the lighting rig.

Spinning around, she covered her mouth with her hand, contemplating the corridor ahead and the options it presented: the lift, Maria's office, the kitchen, or even the cellar.

'Scott. Scott, I have Maria's keys, I found them, we can get out. I'll go and get help!' She called.

Nothing.

She turned her back to the strobe lights and the dancefloor. She moved quickly, one hand on the wall. The light was limited. Past Maria's office, the stairs, the lift door.

Suddenly, darkness.

The hum of the speaker system which had reverberated around the ground floor, stopped!

Silence.

Rosemary froze, then turned and looked back up the corridor.

The towering figure, adorned with a box atop its head stooped forward, casting a silhouette against the bar's light and the intermittent flashes of the strobe.

It swayed in the silence.

'*Rosemary,*' a voice whispered.

It stilled, the beginnings of a horrifying, convulsive motion rippling through its body, contorting its long limbs in a slow, agonising twist. She had seen it before in the temple back in the forest. It surged forward, fluid exploding from beneath the box as it let out a chilling howl.

Stepping away from the safety of the wall and into full view, she started a backward progression.

'You cannot feed off me. Remember? No regrets, no resentment. I'm nothing to you.'

'*Nothing to me. But something to Scott!*'

Roaring, it skittered down the corridor.

She turned. Hand back on the wall again. She ran. Behind her, she heard its body hurtling toward her.

It shrieked.

She kept running. No thought or care. She crashed into the boxes left in the corridor indicating the cellar door.

She burst through it.

Gulping for breath, she fled down the stone steps, hoping she wouldn't lose her footing, wishing her legs weren't so old.

In the cellar, the smell of dampness and beer filled her senses. Her heart still raced and she had only one destination. Behind her, she heard the door to the cellar split apart and the gurgling gasp as Box-Head forced itself down the narrow stone stairs.

Manoeuvring around stainless-steel beer kegs, gas pumps and rubber tubes, Rosemary, at last, found herself at the base of the chute. Light from outside shone through the aged cracks of the wooden hatch. She bent down and carefully began to climb the narrow sticky, stone steps in the centre of the ramp so that she could reach up to the hatch doors.

'*Rosemary,*' The voice behind her hissed.

Rosemary ignored it, her breath laboured shallow gasps. She pushed the hatch door up with a cry of pain as the movement wrenched her arm and climbed up into the light.

Box-Head careened forward shrieking in frustration. Boxes of wine and spirits smashed to the cellar floor. Long black fingers twisted around to form a spike which was thrust forward into the light where Rosemary's hand had been. In one desperate painful movement, Box-Head heaved itself into the light of the outside world.

-43-

Scott rose from his hiding space behind a row of kegs and cylinders. At the edge of the light that now bathed the floor of the cellar, he paused.

'Audiant me vires lucis, terrae et arboris.'

The unfamiliar syllables glided over his lips, carrying with them a sizzling sense of power. Blistering blue, white light around the open hatch pulsed.

'Audiant me vires lucis, terrae et arboris!'

Light faded.

Head lowered, he closed his eyes for a moment. Beyond the hatch, the world was now dark. In the distance, the sounds of the city drifted. He allowed the briefest of smiles then opened his eyes. He turned tail. Footsteps echoed as he ran up the stone steps manoeuvring past the smashed cellar door and back into Euphoria's corridors.

In the women's first-floor restroom, he stepped over Dan's blood and pondered the cubicle at the end. The door looked even more distressed than before.

No time to dwell.

'Scientia proferet viam.' His voice reverberated, and blue-white light appeared. No longer was it contained to the last cubicle. Now it engulfed at least three cubicles and much of the ceiling. A warm wind rushed in from the rift and maple leaves followed, dancing in the current. The wind brushed against his hair and skin. He ignored it, time was ticking. The rift needed to be open fully.

'Scientia proferet viam.'

The light stabilised, and the wind became a breeze and finally disappeared. Leaves came to rest on the surfaces of the room.

What was that in the distance through the light? Like hearing sound from another room, a mournful repetitive wail.

'Shit! Come on Rosemary. Come on!'

***

Rosemary stepped out of the cellar hatch and into a forest.

Delicate flakes floated down and a cold mist swirled around her legs. She shivered. Above her, the familiar blood-red leaves of maple trees formed a dense canopy with only the tiniest pockets of a lilac sky showing through.

Her feet crushed unseen leaves below the mist.

Need to get as much distance between here and the hatch, she thought.

Maple leaves fell and spun about her mockingly as she hurried along, feeling her back tingle at the mere thought of dark fingers reaching out for her flesh.

She broke into a clearing. The glade was open to the sky.

Which way? Her hands steepled.

'Damn it!' she muttered. 'Where's the ridge? The monolith ring?'

Behind her, in the depths of the forest, came a tormented howl. It reverberated around the trees. Box-Head had arrived and the trap was revealed.

It would be after her.

Rosemary ducked behind a tree and mentally reached out to Scott.

'Come on Scott, come on. You must be at the cubicle by now.'

Nothing.

Scott, he'd volunteered as bait to draw the creature back to the forest, but she couldn't allow him to traverse dimensional energy for a third time. Not in such quick succession. The risk was far too dangerous.

Once through the clearing, the trees enveloped her once more.

How can I go faster when all I end up doing is stumbling on tree roots on a surface I can't see? Damn this mist, I'm feeble, slow and old!

She buried her face in her hands.

Box-Head knew this forest, it had been its home, its prison. Unless she got her bearings, it was only a matter of time before it tracked her and caught up.

Trees, trees and more trees. Her head spun from side to side. Was it her imagination or was the landscape changing?

She felt a gentle elevation as she walked. Was this the slight rise she and Scott had gone up together? If it was, it meant she was far from the ridge, the monoliths and the rift.

A blackened ruin came into view, densely smothered with trees.

This was new.

It was a small wooden building, or it had been at some point. A storage shed? Some sort of silo, she thought. The roof had collapsed and the trees themselves had grown up through the ruin.

The trees again, something about the trees – what was it?

A shudder ran through her body as a loud crack followed by a long moaning sound blasted out in the air. The moan was not organic but from some sort of large mechanism. Like pressure or weight applied to an object.

Up through the canopy, the lilac sky had switched to a steelier hue. The mist became a moving mass of cloud that rose rolling across her vision.

Silence.

What was happening?

She dashed to where the side of the ruin was. At least there was some protection. She leaned against the wooden wall, her chest rising and falling.

What was happening?

There was just a white squall and nothing else.

The loud moan erupted again, it was different. The pitch had changed. It steadily became a continuous low resonating hum.

What was that?

A mournful repetitive wail joined the hum from above her – an alarm!

Hands held to her chest, she closed her eyes and reached out to Scott.

Nothing.

With a small cry, she stumbled blindly away.

The mist began to thin and fall back to the forest floor. It was still moving incredibly fast, and still picking up speed, heading in one direction, pulled? Dragged?

And the white flakes were similarly racing through the air.

She passed tree after tree – falling – toppling – swaying like an infant. Her body protested at being pushed so hard and recoiled in pain. Her lower back and hips felt on fire. She came to a halt and stared, bewildered at the mists flowing like water downstream.

Wait! That was it.

The continuous hum.

It suggested a fan, some sort of vacuum. And the sky between the canopy. With a handheld away from her face, her eyes squinting, the sky once again changed. This time from a grey to brilliant white. It was like looking into a fluorescent light in a kitchen.

So many thoughts. What had she learnt about this place?

A fabricated prison set in a pocket of seven seconds. An artificially created environment to maintain a specific type of prisoner.

Her hand fell over her mouth. Now it made sense.

Amidst the hum of the vacuum and the wail of the siren came a sharp hiss that cut through the noise and pulled Rosemary from her thoughts. Her breath rasped in her chest as she turned slowly, blood thumping in her ears. Disorientated, she peered through the trees, into the distance, and a thrashing sound drifted back to her.

Box-Head was tracking her.

She ran.

'Gah!' She crashed to the ground and the cold mist wrapped around her robbing her of breath. She rose, pain shooting through her body, hands grazed and bloody.

Gasping, she slithered behind a big tree and pressed herself against the mossy trunk. She wiped at the perspiration beading on her face now with blood-stained hands.

I hate being old she thought.

It felt like the end. She couldn't go on.

Now she realised how right everyone had been. She was too old for this. Running around like an obsessed child into mystery. At this stage in life, what could she do? Just a stupid old woman with delusions of grandeur, living on the thoughts, memories and feelings of a life now long faded.

What use was she?

She closed her eyes and listened.

Scott's voice floated into her mind.

Rosemary heard Scott talking to someone as if she were listening from a distant room. With his words came a solace that overwhelmed her senses.

'I'm new to all this. It's Rosemary, she stops monsters like Box-Head from coming into our world. A couple of days ago I didn't even know other worlds existed. My life was meaningless. Now I've got a reason to carry on, correct my mistakes, create a better version of myself, help others and live. That's who Rosemary is! Rosemary is risking her life in there because that is what she does – that's who she is! And she is alive and fighting!

Immersed in her emotions, Rosemary slowly blinked her eyes open.

A new perspective rose like bubbles to the surface. Wasn't she doing what she had always done? She was and had made a difference. Yes, she was older but did that mean she was useless?

All her knowledge, experience and wisdom, meant something. It was who she had always been. True to herself through and through and Scott was counting on her, Carol and George back home waiting for her. What words would they whisper to her now if they could? Her age wasn't the issue, it was her perception of her age.

Her eyes filled.

She surveyed to her left through the trees to a small point of light that expanded out irradiating bark, branches and leaves.

Rosemary spun in the direction of the light and ran forward ignoring the pain gathering in her chest and the weight in her legs.

***

A distance behind her in the raging torrent, Box-Head slowly rose from the mist finally sensing movement, or was it something else?

It shrieked, clicked and searched wildly as if unable to see. It convulsed and more thick stringy fluid sprayed from beneath the box. It gave a deep guttural scream and fell once more beneath the swirling rapids.

Moments passed.

A gurgling, feral voice howled.

'*Rosmarrrrrry!*'

The howl blended seamlessly with the unbroken hum and the siren, creating an eerie, unnatural orchestral score.

It had found her.

-44-

The ground rose steadily amidst a deafening screech that reverberated around.

Rosemary pushed it out of her mind.

There through the trees, were the monoliths.

At last, the ridge.

She dug her nails into her dirty hands and tried to ignore the pain and fear shooting through her like electricity.

Another raging screech this time much closer.

Startled, she careered into a small boulder shrouded beneath the fast-flowing mist. She fell heavily to the ground enveloped by the cold milky vapour. Sobbing and in agony, she scrambled up and limped her way forward, checking behind her in intervals.

An ominous creak came from her right.

She ignored it.

Finally, she stepped out of the forest into the clearing with the monoliths and the Dolmen. Of the eight colossal standing stones, one shone, its white light signifying the way home.

Scott had done it.

She let out an uncontrollable cry of joy and staggered forward.

She was going to make it.

'No!' Rosemary cried out in horror.

Only a few more steps.

The white light began to fade. The rift that surrounded the monolith shrank.

Too small.

'God damn you, Scott!' she screamed.

Ignoring the pain, she toppled forward and with bloodied fists, she hammered the boulder's cool hard surface.

***

Click!

The sound came from behind his head.

He had run into the room, avoiding the blood on the floor. Dan's body hadn't been there.

Scott raised both hands.

'Okay, buddy,'

Dan's voice was a slight whisper.

'How about you – you do exactly what I say and close that fucking thing, right now?'

Scott slowly turned.

Dan leant against the frame of one of the cubicles pointing a Glock 17 semi-automatic pistol at him. He raised his free hand to the Glock. Both hands shook, despite his efforts to hide it. There was sweat on his pale brow and his eyes were glazed, his chest labouring with every breath. 'Don't make me use this.' He nodded to the gun in his hand.

The rift light behind Scott began to fade. His heart fell. The light fell back slowly to the last cubicle. His nervous system went into overdrive, fingers tingled as fear flooded his body. He ran through his options. Only one felt instinctive and right.

He breathed out long, slow and lowered both hands.

'It's your choice, Dan, I can't make you use it.

'You can't do this!' Dan yelled. 'That fucking demon is here! It came through, I tried to stop it! I almost did! I can't let you bring more of those things here!'

'That's not what we're doing, Dan. And that creature, the Box-Head, it's back in its realm where it came from,' Scott said, calmly indicating to the remaining blue-white light. 'But Rosemary is back there too. I need to keep the rift open so she–'

'Who the fuck are you two? Rosemary, she... she's just a cleaner, a bloody cleaner!'

'Look mate, you're hurt, you're bleeding out. Lower the gun let me get Rosemary back, then we get you to a hospital.'

'No! No fucking hospital! They said... they said I can't go to any doctors!'

Dan coughed. He spat blood out. 'I'm full of a drug, a drug to infect that demon. If I go to the hospital, I put my family in danger they said. That's what they told me.' A pained smirk grew on his face as he waved the gun frantically. 'That thing may have gotten past me, but it fed– on me– wait till the high dose takes effect.'

'Effect? What happens when it takes effect, Dan? Is Rosemary in even more danger?'

'They said it targets some kind of brain region, intelligence or some shit, I don't know. The fuckers gonna go primal, basic like a dribbling animal.'

Who are they, Dan? Who are you working for, who is making you do–'

'I asked you, who the fuck you two are you?' Dan shouted.

'I'm just someone new to all this. It's Rosemary, she stops creatures like that monster from coming to this world. A couple of days ago I didn't even know other worlds existed. My life didn't mean anything. Now I've got a reason to carry on. I'm going to correct my mistakes, create a better version of myself, help others and live. That's who Rosemary is!'

'You expect me to believe that... that... old woman fights demons?'

'Yes, I do.'

'Let me guess,' Dan said. 'She got fucking superpowers.' He attempted to laugh. Face contorting, his free hand went to his stomach, and he bent over.

Scott drew his brows together. He took a step forward. 'Well, in a way... yes, she does have superpowers and so do I. Those powers are used to stop creatures like Box-Head and that's what I'm going to do. So, if you're going to shoot me, Dan, then shoot me because I'm going to save Rosemary.'

The only sounds were the distant alarm and the sound of their breathing.

A voice sounded somewhere in the club.

'Hello? Is anyone here? Please, anybody?'

'Do you hear that?' Scott pointed to the exit. 'That's one of the women we saved, she's alive.' He slowly indicated behind his shoulder to the last cubicle. 'And Rosemary is risking her life in there because that is what she does – that's who she is! She is alive and fighting, Dan. That sound, can you hear it, that alarm?' He gestured to his ear. 'That alarm on the other side of the rift – it means she hasn't got much time. So, I'm going to turn around and open that rift and help her... so you do what you think is right.'

Scott turned.

'Scientia proferet viam... scientia proferet viam.'

Behind him, he heard Dan breathe out.

'The women, the other women I sent through the cubicle, they aren't coming back, are they? I sent them to their deaths, all of them.'

Hands trembling, Scott turned back around.

Dan's eyes were tightly shut. A twisted expression appeared on his face followed by a painful cry from a blood-filled mouth. He staggered, dropping the gun. Grasping his throat and blood-soaked chest, his knees splayed apart. Dan's face hit the floor, hands not reacting fast enough to stop the fall.

There was a faint, barely perceptible movement of his eyes as a single maple leaf fell across his body.

Dan's body was motionless, his head turned to face the cubicles.

-45-

The final wisps of mist disappeared at the edge of the forest. It revealed a large metal grate embedded in the ground. Rosemary remembered coming across a similar metal grate after Scott had been pulled down beneath the mist.

At least she knew what they were for.

The surface of the cracked monolith sent shivers down her spine as she leaned back against it. Her breathing quickened, she choked and then froze as a lumbering shape approached.

It bent over swaying from side to side, wheezing and groaning. But this was no longer the Box-Head she had fought. The toll of repeatedly passing through dimensional energy had wrought havoc upon Box-Head. It was a grim reminder of the vulnerability non-humans faced in the face of such energies. The once sentient and cognitive being, the Shroud, had regressed into a primal state.

'*Rosemarrrrrry!*' It gurgled stretching out its long fibrous arms.'

Rosemary closed her eyes and mentally reached out. She felt the creature resist the intrusion and then its sounds ceased.

'Your body's saturated with a pathogen. It's changing you, altering you.' She frowned. 'You're not even trying to stop me. Moving through the rift... all that dimensional energy flowing through you... has it caused the virus to accelerate or mutate? Or would the energy have affected you anyway? It affects humans but other beings are not so lucky. Your physiology is different, your very DNA and now you're struggling with basic cognition.'

Her eyes opened.

Box-Head gave out a roar. Its posture contorted, hunching forward, with arms outstretched it began to circle her, obsidian fingers clicking ominously, droplets of saliva glistening at the edges of the box.

Rosemary held her breath and gritted her teeth. It may not be fighting back mentally, but it was still physically strong. Its instincts were those of a predator.

She balled her bloodied hands. Keep it away from me, that's all I need to do.

The pain was like fire. She cringed. It exploded through her causing her vision to blur.

It was almost upon her.

The blistering white sky above the forest suddenly vanished, replaced by an artificial dull ochre. The resonating hum faded away and the last delicate flakes drifted lightly to the ground. The prison guards, Box-Head's people, were alerted to the situation. The environment was compromised. Were all these new occurrences a way of shutting the environment down?

She squeezed her eyes shut and then opened them wide. Rosemary gasped for breath and cried out, unable to hold her mental grip on the creature any longer.

At the same moment, a small white light grew from behind her. It expanded, casting her shadow over Box-Head like some giant blanket.

Box-Head howled, it spun cowering.

Rosemary rolled onto all fours, don't black out, don't black out! With a scream, she pushed herself to her feet.

A second white light erupted from the dolmen metres away. She squinted. The lights from both the cracked monolith and the Dolmen pulsed. They were growing brighter humming like a generator. At last, they stabilised.

As she took a step into the light. Sounds, whispers, and muffled voices rang in her ears, it was from the Dolmen. It's towering presence, marked by three imposing standing stones and a colossal flat stone crowning the structure, drew her attention. With its steady luminous aura an unmistakable gateway, an entrance to another realm, clearly visible, serving as a doorway from the Shroud's world. One thing was clear, the jailors of Box-Head... the Shroud were coming.

'*Home.*'

The voice whispered in her head as she tottered forward, consumed in pure white light.

Was that Box-Head knelt like a man in prayer? A vision?

Several tall figures stood on either side of it clothed in ebony medieval-style robes and cowls.

'*I know of your home, Rosemarrrrrrrry,*' the voice hissed, '*and now, even more, will know of it.*'

The image faded.

The world became white.

***

'Rosemary! Rosemary?'

Scott's voice sounded distant. Her eyes fluttered open.

Relief washed over his face, yet she sensed despite it, he couldn't overlook her physical pain, injuries and exhaustion.

The room shook, there was a rumble far off in the club and the emergency lights flickered.

Rosemary's eyes widened.

'What's happening? Did we do it?' She coughed.

'You look like shit. Yeah, the rift's closed. You're bleeding!'

She closed her eyes. 'It's gone. Box-Head... there's nothing.' She turned back to the last cubicle. 'I'm alright, I barely made it. What happened? Why did the rift close?'

'Dan pulled a gun on me, he wasn't so dead. I think paralysed or something but when he came around his injuries...'

'Like a spider paralysing prey – storing it for later,' Rosemary whispered.

'You were just standing there after you came through the cubicle. It must have been thirty seconds... in a sort of trance, I managed to close the rift and...'

Rosemary held up a hand and scanned the floor. Reaching down, she picked up a maple leaf.

'maple trees. maple trees. I'm missing something, something important,' she said. 'There were mature, fully grown maple trees in that forest?' Her finger pointed back at the cubicle. 'Maples are native to North America. We grow them in every garden across the world. How did they get to an artificial environment in another dimension?'

A few seconds passed. A dreadful thought surfaced. She steadied herself on the sink.

'Rosemary?'

'They've been here before,' she whispered.

Dust fell from the ceiling tiles as the room shook again.

She reached out gripping Scott. Pain shot through her arm.

More dust fell from above.

'Oh, you have got to be kidding me! I thought I was imagining it!' Rosemary shouted.

Scott shook his head. 'It started just after I closed the rift. We need to get out now. Jax is awake too, she's outside I asked her to stay in the corridor, I didn't want her to see Dan's body again.'

'Good...Good thinking, luv.'

They headed for the restroom door but Rosemary's knees sagged and her hand went to her chest. A strong arm caught her in time.

'Jax, I need you!' Scott shouted.

The restroom door burst open and Jax stood holding open the door.

'She's here? You found her! Wait, what the hell happened?'

'She'll be okay but we have to go now!'

'But what about the creature that attacked me?'

'I told you, Jax, he's gone, now we-'

'Give her to me.'

Jax had stepped forward ignoring the horror of the room. Rosemary felt an arm wrap around her.

'Lean on me, I'm stronger than I look and I need a distraction!'

Rosemary didn't argue.

As Scott held open the door, Rosemary grabbed his arm.

'The bags, my radio, they're in the cleaning cupboard. We can't leave without them.'

'I'll get them. Jax, get Rosemary to the top of the stairs – go!'

With one final look back at the cubicle at the end and the shrivelled body on the floor, they left the room.

Rosemary ignored the pain and held onto Jax, together they struggled to the top of the stairs.

'You're stronger than you look, and brave,' Rosemary mumbled.

'My mom's a nurse. She taught me and my brother how to lift properly – said it would come in useful one day.'

'Smart mother.'

'And let's face it, I've been drugged – gone unconscious – I've woken up in a forest – attacked by... whatever the hell that thing was – and knocked unconscious again! I'm running on adrenaline right now.'

Rosemary sensed movement but it was only Scott. He ran up to them.

'I've got the bags and the radio,' Scott said. 'Let's go before this place collapses. It must be residual feedback from the rift. This part of the club is only just holding up, but I doubt it'll be for much longer.'

Rosemary peered at him. 'How do you know that? Never mind.'

They made their way down to the ground floor.

Another tremor.

Something crashed onto the dancefloor.

The building groaned.

Another tremor, glass smashed behind the bars.

'The cellar – quickly!'

Another loud groan.

They manoeuvred through the smashed cellar door.

Lights flickered continuously now.

Jax went through first and descended the stone stairs. Rosemary followed using the walls and Scott to steady her.

'Which way now?' Jax screamed.

'Over there, you'll see a hatch,' Rosemary gasped.

They clambered gingerly up the narrow cold stone steps and out into a cool fresh night.

They moved passed bins and empty crates. Rosemary caught sight of Maria's ebony BMW.

They headed through two large gates and down the side of Euphoria.

Roof tiles fell, crashing about them like hail.

An ear-splitting sound of metal under stress reverberated. A final boom sounded from somewhere deep inside the club.

Nearby dogs began to bark and alarms rang out in protest into the night sky.

Euphoria's luminous sign fizzled and spat before finally going out.

***

Scott slammed the van door.

'We need to get you two to a hospital.' Scott started the engine.

A hand rested on his arm.

'Not so fast sunshine. We can't go to a hospital – too many questions. I know a doctor we can go to. I trust her – wait... damn! My phone, I must have left it at home. It doesn't matter... I know where she lives, I'll direct you. Is that okay with you, Jax?'

Through the driver's mirror, Scott saw Jax nod.

'My friend Amy...' Jax said.

'I'm sorry, luv,' whispered Rosemary.

The van pulled out and disappeared into the city lights.

-46-

Scott trudged into his empty cold apartment. Kicking off his shoes, he tossed his keys into the flowerpot.

Switching on the heat, he awkwardly filled a kettle before lumbering into his bedroom. Gently, he removed his clothes and stepped into the bathroom, ran the shower and got in.

For a long time, the water ran down the tiles.

Did all that happen? Was it real?

The understanding of his past, and the memories of Phaedrus that were now a part of him. The people killed by Box-Head. They would never see their families or friends again! No more Christmas, birthdays or holidays. Feelings of sunlight on the skin, experiencing a kiss, being held in someone's arms... all gone.

Scott shook himself.

Wrapping his dressing gown around him, he walked into the bedroom. It was now raining outside, hitting the glass and running down. He stepped to the window, closed his eyes and pressed his forehead to the cold surface relishing the sensation.

Two delicate arms wrapped around him.

'Hello, you,' said Annie.

He chuckled.

She hugged him gently aware of his injury then let go and stood back.

Scott turned. 'Hello, Annie.'

'Well look at you,' she teased before unceremoniously dropping onto the bed. She bounced with a soft laugh and rolled onto her front to get herself into position to raise herself on her elbows.

'I said you were going to be something special, but I never thought it was going to happen so fast.'

'Am I that different? Even from this morning?' he asked taking a step forward.

She raised herself higher, meeting his gaze with her big brown eyes. 'You're clearly not the same man as before' she replied. 'Can you tell me what happened?'

Scott grinned 'No, not just yet.'

She rolled over like a child, grabbed the sheets and peeked up at him.

'You don't have to be afraid of me. I'd be more afraid of the rain if I were you.'

'You're the girl who had a thing for me, before my fugue, the memory loss, right? The one who trailed me in every nightclub while I was dealing. You'd never touched drugs, not once. But then you did, just so I'd pay attention to you. How could I have forgotten you, Annie? I'm so sorry. I remember everything now.'

'I thought at the time... if I could just get you to see me, like me and maybe go on a date then I could get you away from all that. Funny, but I now realise that would never have happened. You needed to make that decision for yourself. Seems such a long time ago. I had a huge crush on you, and I think I always will. Your face floated in my mind as I faced death. In those last moments, my thoughts weren't with my parents or my life, they were filled with the hope that this may be the thing to make you walk away from it all. Strange, I imagined being around to witness it happen.'

Scott stepped over to the bed and swept Annie up in his arms, tears streamed down his face.

'I'm so sorry, so sorry I did this to you, your family, your life. I wasn't there for you or my mom and dad, I was selfish and...'

'Hush now. Hush. You were in a dark place.' She pulled back clasping her hands around his tear-stained cheeks. 'Are you still in a dark place?'

'No,' he sniffed. 'I'm in a fantastic place considering. I'm overwhelmed with a hell of a lot of making up I have to do.' He smiled. 'And I got the memories of some old Greek guy in my head called Phaedrus Castellanos.' He chuckled wiping his nose on his sleeve.

'A new friend of sorts then, like the cleaning lady? Someone you can trust.'

'You mean Rosemary. Hell, she's no cleaning lady,'

Annie's eyes narrowed. 'I can also see that you're wondering where to go with all this?'

'Yeah.'

'Don't worry, you have plenty of time. We... have plenty of time.'

'Annie?'

'Yes?'

'You died, but you're here.'

'So...'

'Based on my newfound knowledge and experience,' he wiped his eyes, 'are you a ghost?'

'And finally, the penny drops!' She punched the air before falling backwards onto the bed.

'I mean... ghosts exist, how... I mean, how long can you stay for?'

'Long enough, but not forever. Can't leave you at the start of your adventures, can I? Let's just say that I'm a sucker for guys with long hair. Now go and get something to eat. You look like shit.'

He sighed with a smile. 'This will take some getting used to, my very own ghost.'

He felt her brown eyes watching him as he rose and headed for the bedroom door.

'I'll click the kettle on again,' he said.

She didn't answer, she had turned away towards the window transfixed for a moment at the rain running down the window. She frowned.

Scott headed for the kitchen.

***

Rosemary stood outside the wooden gate of her house. She looked down and examined the palms of her hands. The grazes were gone and so were the bruises all over her body.

Her legs, her back, her arm... all healed. She simply smiled before rummaging through her bag to retrieve her keys.

Inside, she locked the front door and looked around. She waited... and then it came.

'Mom, is that you? What time do you call this?' Carol shouted down from upstairs, 'Betty's been calling for you and left a message.'

'What did she say, luv?'

'Something about the plumber and not to go there. He's no good. What's it all about Mom?'

'Nothing, luv. Just stuff with the social club. I'll give her a call before I go to bed.'

'It sounded urgent!'

'Yes, luv. I know. Don't worry, I'll call her,' Rosemary replied, removing her coat.

She wandered into the kitchen, switched the kettle on, searched a cupboard and walked into the lounge, holding a packet of malted milk biscuits. She stared down at her dirty clothes and blew out a long breath. Fishing her battered radio out of her bag, she wiped a loving hand over it.

She sat in her favourite chair for a while staring at the wall clock then hid the radio back in the depths of her knitting bag.

Her eyes felt heavy.

Above her in Carol's room, she heard the muffled sound of a TV.

The normality of it all.

Everything was as it should be.

Her eyes closed.

Sleep came.

Two days later

Scott pondered the bruises on his arm, put down his mug of tea and looked around.

The whiteboard advertised the meal of the day; cod, chips and peas. The milk steamer hissed, drowning out multiple conversations. The till sprang open. Together with the clatter of cups and plates, the atmosphere was more comforting than at any other time in his life. It all implied normality, but now it was forever changed. The world is perceived through a new set of glasses and reality is sharpened.

'Hey sunshine, snap out of it,' Rosemary laughed.

Scott turned but he couldn't smile. 'I'm still waiting for your explanation of your miraculous recovery. The cuts, bruises on your hands, the limp, the pain. Now look at you, it's like none of that happened but I know you were pretty knocked about after the forest.'

'What can I say? I have good genetics,' Rosemary replied suddenly fascinated with the surface of her latte.

'You're not telling me everything. And you're not going to tell me, are you?'

She just looked up, a twinkle in her eye.

'Rosemary, how can you be so... so easy about all this? I'm not just talking about your recovery, I mean everything we went through.'

She took a sip of her latte. 'Experience,' she replied.

He shrugged. 'Just look at them,' he indicated to the people in the café.

The old man in the flat cap, hypnotically stirring his coffee; three women, who danced their forks over cake wanting to give the impression they could dismiss it but secretly happy to eat it because it would be terribly unsocial not to. Two lads with precariously balanced baseball caps like vultures bent over a corpse staring at their phone screens and the owner, an overweight middle-aged man with the dress sense of someone who clearly loved the 1980s.

'They have no clue, do they? None of them? Those women died,' Scott whispered leaning forward. 'We know what happened and we can't say a single thing.'

'I know, luv.'

'Their families will always wonder where they are, expecting them to show up at the front door one day.'

'We stopped it. No more young women can be taken and no more lives will be lost.'

'Yeah, I know, I know.' He took a sip from his cup.

'Wars, terrorist attacks, the public never hear about the hundreds that are prevented. It's all kept quiet; people are kept ignorant so they can go about their daily lives. Wheels keep turning, factories run and money moves.'

'It seems unfair,' Scott huffed. 'We did what we did, and nobody will know.'

'Not being able to tell anyone about what we do is one of the hardest things about the job. It's why it's so important, vital even, to have others like us in our lives.'

He felt her a hand over his. The rings on her fingers caught the sunlight and gleamed.

'My Henry said to me, on many an occasion I might add, that it would get easier, working with the paranormal weird stuff,' she laughed, 'and he was right, it does and it will. I do believe that you were sent to me for a reason. I genuinely believe that. Something is happening, something big and you being here now just proves it. You have a remarkable ability, Scott. Work with me.'

She released his hand.

'Work with you?'

'Work with me. Moon and Finn Paranormal Investigations, what do you think? Hey, don't look so horrified, I'm not retiring yet!'

'No, It... It's just I didn't expect it.'

'Come on... you want answers, right? You have the memories of Phaedrus Castellanos, whoever he was, which

I may say has got a contact of mine extremely excited. You may be able to solve an awfully long mystery.'

'A cold case?'

Rosemary took another sip of her latte. 'It is looking that way, yes.'

'I can tell you this, Phaedrus had a thing for the British red telephone box,' Scott chuckled.

'Really? Now that is interesting, red phone boxes play a significant role in the paranormal world.' She placed her mug down. 'Oh, by the way before I forget, I spoke to some medical acquaintances of mine about the condition your consultant diagnosed.'

'The fugue state?'

'Yes, they were able to fill me in on psychogenic fugues or dissociative amnesia.'

'Mouthful isn't it,' Scott said.

'Fugues are indeed rare. The most marked characteristic is the loss of personal information.'

'And I gather you also know that it's usually associated with a traumatic or emotional event?' Scott drew patterns on the tablecloth with his teaspoon.

He felt her hand on his again.

'Yes, they did, and it does. Emotional trauma and repressed memories harm the conscious mind. The fugue is considered a defence mechanism. It makes sense.'

'I guess.'

'How does that make you feel?'

Scott arched an eyebrow. 'Honestly, I'm terrified. And on top of that, I've got all these paranormal abilities now.'

She withdrew her hand. 'This is why you need me around. You and I working together, cracking cases, all sounds good to me. 'Who better to train you than me?

'Yeah, yeah, okay you can train me. But hey! Won't you be getting another cleaning job?'

He saw her eyes widen.

'I'm not a bloody cleaner! I was undercover. I sense rifts and I find them, cheeky sod!'

'Oops, sorry.' He spun the teaspoon in his fingers. 'Anything back yet about the syringes and needles?' He asked.

'No. Nothing. Still waiting on it.' Rosemary set about turning the laminated menu over. 'You know when you said that you sensed Box-Head in your dreams. I think that was just you, flexing your psychic muscles. I don't think it knew too much about you, but that's why you were aware of it.'

'That explains the dreams.'

'That it does.'

'Anything from Jax?' Scott asked.

'No nothing since the doctor we went to. She's a smart girl though, I think she'll be okay, hope we see her again.'

Taking the last swig of his tea, Scott got to his feet and made his way over the counter to pay. All the glass, chrome and cutlery in the room caught the light as the sun shone through the large window. It cast a glow across the people, surfaces and walls.

As Scott waited for the receipt, he spied Rosemary watching the customers, a smile on her face. She gathered her coat and bag and joined him at the counter.

'So, how's it going with your parents?' She asked, dapping her eye with a handkerchief.

'Good so far with Mom and Dad. They're understandably cautious. I've got a lot of making up and trust to earn.'

At that moment, the café door swung open and a man bustled in. As he entered, bringing a gust of leaves blew across the floor. Scott bent down and picked up... a fresh green leaf.

'Yes, luv. Give them time,' Rosemary said. 'You're their son, they love you. It's part of the job of being a parent.

He handed Rosemary the mint green leaf.

She smiled glancing down at the leaf. 'Yes, we're both back, aren't we? And do you know what?? I don't think I'm ready to give up sticking my nose in where it doesn't belong.

Not just yet. And as for you, sunshine, it's fair to say you've turned over a new leaf too.'

'Oh! You just had to get that one in, didn't you?'

'How could I not.'

'Finn and Moon Paranormal Investigations.'

'Moon and Finn,' Rosemary replied. 'I've already done the letterheads.'

'You knew I was going to say yes.'

Rosemary smiled.

He grinned. 'I think I'm going to regret this partnership but...' he breathed out deeply, 'But I think I can handle this.'

'Yes, Scott, I have full confidence in you and with Phaedrus lending a hand, we're all set.' Her smile radiated as she tucked the leaf into her coat pocket.

They walked out, leaving behind the smell of coffee and bacon, the hiss of the milk steamer, the clatter of crockery and dancing light on walls.

The End

Guy M Etchells belongs to The New Street Authors, an indie publishing collective based in England. Among his works, *A Window Cracked*, a short story featured in the New Street Stories Anthology, shares a universe with his first novel, *The Cubicle at the End*.

Residing in central England, Guy is an ardent enthusiast of sci-fi, fantasy, and the MARVEL universe.

For more information please visit guyetchells.com

Acknowledgements

To David Wake, Lucy Brisbane and Marie Phipps for their invaluable feedback, insightful suggestions and neverending encouragement during the writing process.

To Sean Strong (seanstrong.com) for his amazing cover design that perfectly captures the essence of the story.

And to all my readers now and in the future, thank you for embarking on this journey with me.

Printed in Great Britain
by Amazon